MURDER ON THE EAST COAST

A Cedar Bay Cozy Mystery - Book 10

BY

DIANNE HARMAN

Published by: Dianne Harman
www.dianneharman.com

Interior, cover design and website by
Vivek Rajan
www.RewireYourDNA.com

ISBN: 978-1537246161

CONTENTS

ACKNOWLEDGMENTS

As always, thank you, my loyal readers, for taking the time to read the books I write! Obviously, I love writing them, and I'm so glad you seem to enjoy reading them. Think it's called a win-win situation! This is book number ten in the popular Cedar Bay Cozy Mystery Series featuring Kelly and Sheriff Mike Reynolds. I hope you like it as much as you've enjoyed the books in my other four cozy mystery series, Liz Lucas, High Desert, Midwest, and Jack Trout. Because of you, every one of my books has received Amazon's prestigious "bestseller" gold flag. I'm truly humbled and honored. Thanks again!

This book came about as a result of a trip to Virginia to attend a graduation ceremony and see a friend of mine, Jackie Ritacco, receive her doctorate degree. Yes, I became a believer in she crab soup and lobster rolls after the trip, and yes, I did visit Boston and York, Maine. It was a fascinating trip and took me to places I'd never before visited. Funny aside – my husband read the prologue of the book and said, "Oh no, you can't have Jackie murdered. I play golf with her husband!" I assured him the victim was not our friend, Jackie, but instead another graduate.

This novel is a book of fiction, so therefore it's a figment of my imagination, but that imagination was fueled by the graduation I saw and the places I visited!

As always, thanks to Vivek who creates fabulous covers and patiently prepares my books for final publication. And to Tom, my husband, who gives me ideas for books and catches mistakes I somehow never saw! I totally rely on both of them. Thanks, gentlemen!

And as I usually do, I need to thank my dog, Kelly, for her ability to constantly keep me amused and finally, thank heavens, learning to play by herself. Rolling a ball down the stairs, running down to get it, bringing it to the top of the stairs, and doing it all over again can keep her busy for hours! Thanks, Kelly!

Kindle & Ebooks for FREE

Go to www.dianneharman.com/freepaperback.html and get your FREE copies of Dianne's books and Dianne's favorite recipes immediately by signing up for her newsletter.

Once you've signed up for her newsletter you're eligible to win a Kindle. One lucky winner is picked every week. Hurry before the offer ends.

PROLOGUE

It was a beautiful sunny Virginia day when Julie Jensen proudly stepped across the outdoor stage at the graduation ceremony and accepted her DSL, Doctor of Strategic Leadership, diploma from the dean of the Business School. She waved it above her head as she left the stage, red hair streaming out from under her cap, grinning at the applause from the huge crowd cheering on the graduates. It was a dream come true, the culmination of years of thinking about the diploma she now held in her hand. She knew her life would never be the same, but what she didn't know was she only had hours to live.

CHAPTER ONE

"Ladies and gentlemen, this is Captain Westin from the flight deck. I'm sorry for any inconvenience this may cause you, but we're going to have to make an emergency landing in Knoxville, Tennessee. We have a de-icing problem with the plane which shouldn't take long to fix. I promise you we'll be back in the air in no time. Thanks for your patience!"

"Well, this is a first," Kelly said. "I've never been to Knoxville before, but judging by all the green fields I can see below us, it looks like they get plenty of rain."

"Nor have I," Mike said. "I wonder how long we're going to be delayed. I'm glad the graduation ceremony is tomorrow and not tonight, or we probably wouldn't make it."

"After Steph has worked so hard to get her DSL, and was so excited we were going to be at her graduation along with her family, I think she'd really be disappointed if we didn't make it because of a mechanical failure on our plane. Every time I tell people a fifty-five-year-old friend of mine is getting a doctorate, they can't believe it."

"Yeah, it's a pretty big deal. Wonder how Rich is going to feel about her making dinner reservations in the name of Dr. and Mr. Rocco."

"I think he's just happy she's finished with it. Working full time, being married, and trying to earn a doctorate degree, had to be exhausting for her, and I'm sure it wasn't easy for him. They're going to Mexico a couple of days after she graduates for a little R and R time, and I think they both deserve it. She wanted to go directly from here, but she has to make some big presentation in Portland on Monday at the company where she works."

"This is Captain Westin again. I've just been notified we'll be changing planes when we land, and as soon as all the luggage has been transferred, we'll be back in the air. Please stay in the lounge area close to the gate, so we can leave promptly. Thank you."

"That's encouraging. We probably have time for a coke, and that's about it. I wasn't looking forward to spending the night in the airport terminal," Mike said as he followed Kelly down the aisle of the plane and into the terminal waiting area.

True to the Captain's word, thirty minutes later their flight was announced over the PA system, and they boarded the replacement plane and continued on their way to Norfolk, Virginia. The trip was short, and even though they landed an hour later than planned, it was still light out. They retrieved their luggage from the baggage carousel and then walked to the nearby rental car booth. Fifteen minutes later they were on their way to the hotel which was located on the university campus and where they'd be staying for the next two days.

"Wow! I had no idea the university was large enough to have its own hotel on the campus. I don't think I've ever seen that before. Stephanie told me she had to make our reservations really far in advance, and now I can see why. I imagine everyone wants to stay in this hotel on graduation weekend," Kelly exclaimed as she looked out the car window at the large beautifully landscaped campus.

"What about dinner tonight? Are we meeting Stephanie and Rich?"

"No. I texted her when we had the de-icing problem in Knoxville. I wasn't sure how long we'd be there, and I didn't want them to wait for us. Think we made it here just in time. It's starting to get dark and driving around in a new area is always a little difficult. Let's check in and then find a place to eat. I'm starving!" Kelly said.

They walked through the hotel lobby to the reception desk, passing by several placards indicating in which rooms private graduation parties were being held.

"Welcome to the Plantation Inn," the beautiful dark haired young woman said in a heavy southern drawl. "Y'all here for the graduation?"

"Yes, a friend of ours is graduating tomorrow. We're from Oregon."

"Must be a good friend to come all that way. You can pick up a map over there that'll show you how to get to the graduation ceremony tomorrow morning. It's not far from here. And your name?"

"Mike and Kelly Reynolds."

"I don't see those exact names, but I do have a Sheriff and Mrs. Mike Reynolds."

"That would be us," Kelly said. "By the way, I'm starving. I'm assuming you have a restaurant here."

"We do, but there are so many parties here tonight it closed early. The kitchen was just plain overwhelmed by all the catering jobs, but the pub is open, and you can get a sandwich there."

"That will do just fine. We'll put our luggage in our room and be back in a few minutes. Could you point us in the right direction?" Mike asked.

"Pub's down that hall. When you get to the end take a left. You can't miss it. Personally, I think the hamburger is really good."

"You've sold me. A few French fries on the side, and I'll be happy," Kelly said smiling at the young woman as she returned Mike's credit card to him. The receptionist handed them a map of the hotel and circled where their room was located.

After they finished registering, they walked back to where Mike had parked their rental car in the hotel parking lot. "Kelly, I think we'll take our bags directly to the room. The parking lot's so crowded I don't think I'll be able to find a spot closer to our room, and I'd sure hate to lose the one I have. Matter of fact, with the looks of all the parties being held here tonight, I think we were lucky to find this one."

An hour and a half later, full of hamburgers and french fries, they went to bed looking forward to the next day and the upcoming graduation. They both slept soundly, not knowing that less than twenty-fours later they would begin a search for a killer.

CHAPTER TWO

The next morning after they had their coffee, showered, and gotten dressed, Kelly said, "Mike, I just got a text from Stephanie. She has to report early to the staging area with the other graduates and said we should meet Rich and the rest of her family in the lobby. We can walk to the graduation ceremony from there."

"Give me two minutes. I need to finish this email. Evidently yesterday was pretty eventful in Beaver County. Not only was there a major traffic accident, but there were also reports of several burglaries, all of them in county territory and under my jurisdiction. I told my deputy I'd meet him at the office as soon as our plane lands Sunday. Actually, I think I better see if we can get an earlier flight."

"Well, try not to let it spoil today. I know we're here for Steph's graduation, but you deserve a little break from work. I'm sure your deputies can handle things in your absence."

"You sound a lot more confident than I feel," he said, putting his phone in his pocket and walking towards the door. "Let's go."

*****

It was a beautiful late Spring day, sunny and warm. Thousands of people waited expectantly for the graduates to cross the stage and pick up their diplomas, which assured them that they had indeed earned a degree. Mike and Kelly sat with Rich and the rest of Stephanie's family, her sister, son, daughter, and granddaughter. When Stephanie crossed the stage to pick up her diploma, all of them yelled and clapped as loudly as they could. They repeated the process a few minutes later when Stephanie's friend, Julie Jensen, accepted hers.

Rich leaned over and said to Kelly, "I'm sure Julie appreciated that. You know Stephanie met her through the DSL program here at the university, and when she decided to divorce her husband, Stephanie convinced her to move to Portland and work in her company. Julie had been doing similar work for a company like Stephanie's, so it was an easy transition for her. Unfortunately, we're all she has here at the graduation. Her mother's in very ill health, Julie's going through a divorce, she doesn't have any children, and I guess her brother's a real good-for-nothing. I'm glad we included her in the celebration dinner we're going to have tonight."

"I'm looking forward to meeting her," Kelly said. "Stephanie's told me so much about her. I'm glad we could be here to support her and Stephanie. This is a pretty big deal for both of them."

"You bet it is," Brigette, Stephanie's daughter said, laughing. "Now I can have my mom back, and she can babysit for me."

"Actually, I'm looking forward to having my golfing partner back," Rich chimed in. "Trust me, it's been a long three years, but I have to say I'm really proud of her. I was playing around on the Internet one day, and I tried to look up the percent of people in the United States who hold doctoral degrees, but I never did find anything definitive. The only thing I came away with is that it really is a big deal!"

"Rich, text us and let us know what time dinner is tonight," Mike said. We're going to have lunch in Virginia Beach at a place called Bubba's. Yeah, I know, you never want to play poker with a guy named Doc, you never eat breakfast at a place called Mom's, and you sure don't eat lunch at a place called Bubba's when you're in the South," Mike said with a smile on his face.

He was interrupted by Rich who was looking at him in disbelief. "You're kidding, of course. I'd never eat at any place called Bubba's."

"No, Rich, he's not kidding," Kelly said. "I checked out all of the reviews, and this place is supposed to have the best she crab soup and crab cakes in all of Virginia. One of Mike's deputies told him he couldn't come to this part of the United States and not eat at Bubba's, so we'll see you later. Tell Stephanie how proud we are of her." With that, she and Mike stood up and walked towards the rear of the crowd as they headed back to their hotel room and then on to lunch.

*****

"There it is, Mike. Pull into that narrow driveway. I hope the food is better than their signage. We almost missed it."

"From the number of cars in the parking lot, we're not the only ones who read about Bubba's, or maybe these are the locals. Actually, I hope that's the case. The locals always know where the best places are to eat."

As they walked up the steps of the waterfront restaurant they saw some fishing boats in the water on the far side of the restaurant. "May I help you?" the young waiter asked.

"Yes, two for lunch."

"Would you like to eat on the patio or inside?"

"Mike, I'd like to eat inside," Kelly said. "I'm still hot after sitting in the sun during the graduation. Air conditioning sounds just fine to me right now."

"Please follow me," the young man said as he led them to a table with a view of the fishing boats bobbing up and down in the estuary next to the restaurant. He saw them looking out at the boats and said, "Yes, that's how fresh our catches are. You can watch while they unload them. Your waiter will be with you in a moment."

They looked at the menus the waiter brought, although both of them had decided before they'd even entered the restaurant that they were going to have she crab soup and crab cakes. When the waiter brought their soup, Kelly sipped a spoonful and said, "Now I know why people rave about this. I don't know if I could ever make anything close to this at the coffee shop, but I sure would like to try. This is fantastic."

"Couldn't agree more. By the way, Kelly, you told me once, but I've forgotten. I know you and Stephanie lived next door to each other when you were growing up, and then she moved to Portland. How did you get from her moving to Portland to coming here for her graduation?"

"Even though Stephanie was a year older than me, we were always good friends. After high school, she left for college, and I stayed in Cedar Bay and helped my parents run Kelly's Koffee Shop. I got married, had two children, and became a widow. She got married twice, had two children, and raised them after her second divorce. She worked full time in the health care industry. She always loved to learn and even with her children and working full time, she managed to get a master's degree in health care.

"No matter what was going on in our lives, we always talked to each other by phone at least once a week. About five years ago she started telling me she wished she'd gone on and gotten a doctorate. I told her it wasn't too late. We went back and forth a lot about it. She'd recently married Rich and was afraid it wouldn't be fair to her new husband to take on something like that, but the one thing she kept harping on was that she was just too old to do it. She said by the time she got her degree she'd be in her mid-fifties. I remember telling her once that she was going to be in her mid-fifties anyway, so she might as well have her degree when she got there."

Kelly stopped talking as the waiter cleared their soup bowls and served them the crab cakes they'd ordered. Mike took a bite and said, "Don't even try to duplicate these. They are simply wonderful. Bet it has something to do with being on the East Coast. Think they'd lose some essential taste if they were frozen and had to travel across the country."

"You're probably right. I'm just glad to have the chance to experience them. The bar these set would probably be too hard to exceed. Think this will have to be just a good memory. Anyway, let me wrap this up about Stephanie. During one of our conversations I told her if she got her doctorate, I'd fly back here to Virginia and attend her graduation. She never let me forget it, and of course, I had to do it. By the way, glad you were so easy to convince."

"Knowing you as I do, Kelly, I doubt Stephanie ever considered that you wouldn't keep your promise. Actually, this part of the country is all new to me, and I'm enjoying it. It's a good thing we're going home tomorrow, because I'd probably spend all my time and money right here in this restaurant stuffing myself with nothing but she crab soup and crab cakes."

"Don't know about you, Sheriff, but it's been a long morning, and I'm also stuffed. I could be talked into going back to the hotel and napping before we have to meet the group for dinner."

"Music to my ears, sweetheart," he said as he motioned for the waiter to bring the bill.

An hour later they were both sound asleep, the white noise of the air conditioner muffling the nearby graduation celebration sounds. Later, they'd look back on that nap as the quiet before the storm, the storm of murder.

CHAPTER THREE

"Mike, wake up. I got a text from Stephanie a little while ago that says we're supposed to meet all of them for dinner in the dining room in an hour. Thought you might want to take a shower first," Kelly said.

"Definitely. After sitting in the sun at graduation and sleeping for a couple of hours, that sounds good. You want to go first, or do you want me to?"

"Go ahead. There's a mirror here in the room, and I can use it to refresh my makeup. Think I'll pass on a shower, because I really don't want to spend time doing my hair again."

Her phone rang just as Mike stepped out of the bathroom, a towel wrapped around his waist. Kelly picked it up and listened for a moment, then she said in a somber voice, "Stephanie, start at the beginning. Tell me what's happened. I'm going to put you on speakerphone, so Mike can hear as well."

"Rich went to Julie's room to see if she wanted to join us for a glass of champagne to celebrate our graduation. When he got to her room, the door was open. He called out to her, but she didn't answer. He walked in and found her lying on the floor in a pool of blood. She was ddeeaad," Stephanie sobbed. "Please, can you and Mike come to our room? It's number 35, just down the walkway from yours. The police are on their way. I've never had to deal with anything like this. I knew something like this was going to happen. I just knew it. I didn't want to tell anybody, but it was in the stars."

"We'll be there in two minutes. Is Rich with you now?" Kelly asked.

"Yes, he knocked on the door next to Julie's, told the people what had happened, and asked them to call security and notify the police. A security guard is standing outside her room waiting for them. As soon as the guard got there, Rich came back to the room to tell me. Please hurry. I know Mike can talk to the police a lot better than we can."

"Stephanie, this is Mike. We'll be there in a couple of minutes. Just stay where you are."

Kelly ended the call, and they both dressed as quickly as possible. Five minutes later they were knocking on Stephanie's door. She opened it immediately and fell into Kelly's hug.

"Rich, tell me everything you can think of before the police come," Mike said, "and let me caution you both to only answer the questions you're asked by them. Don't give any additional information. I know you had nothing to do with this, but at this point, the less said the better. Trust me on this."

Rich, who was clearly shaken, took a deep breath and began, "Steph and I bought a bottle of champagne this afternoon and thought it would be nice for the two of us to celebrate before the family dinner tonight. I walked over to Julie's room to see if she wanted to join us, and that's when I found her. It looked like she'd been shot in the chest."

"Okay, I hear some sirens in the distance. Let me ask you a couple of quick questions. Did you see a murder weapon in the room?"

"Not that I recall," Rich answered.

Mike turned to Stephanie and asked, "Did Julie usually wear jewelry?"

"Yes, her mother is quite wealthy and has given her a lot of jewelry over the years. She always wore a diamond pendant on a gold chain, a gold and amethyst bracelet, diamond stud earrings, and a large diamond ring on her right hand. She stopped wearing her wedding ring when she and Mark separated. Why?"

"Rich, try and remember if Julie was wearing any jewelry when you saw her."

Mike recognized the classic sign of someone trying to remember something, as Rich looked up and off to his left. A moment later he said, "She must have been wearing her earrings, because I had a thought that diamonds and blood don't belong together. I don't remember seeing any other jewelry on her, but I probably was somewhat in a state of shock. I really can't say with any certainty what jewelry, if any, she was wearing."

They heard a knock on the door accompanied by a loud voice saying, "Police, please open the door."

"I'll get it, Stephanie," Mike said reaching the door in two long strides. The policeman standing at the door was wearing a police uniform with four stars on his shirt collar. Mike recognized the stars which indicated he was the chief of police.

"Chief, please come in. My name is Sheriff Mike Reynolds," he said, holding out his hand and giving his identification to the police chief.

The chief shook his hand and said, "Must not be from around here, Sheriff. I don't recognize you, and I've been with the force long enough to know pretty much everyone involved in law enforcement." He looked at Mike's identification. "Guess I was right."

"You are. I'm the sheriff in Beaver County, Oregon. My wife and I are here in Virginia for our friend Stephanie's graduation," he said, nodding towards Stephanie who was sitting on the bed weeping with Rich's arm around her.

"You must be Rich Rocco, and you must be Mrs. Rocco. I'm Police Chief Ken Anders. I was told the person that discovered the body was a registered guest staying in this room. Several of my deputies are at the scene of the crime, looking for evidence. The coroner's on his way. He'll conduct his examination and release the body to a local mortuary. Has the next of kin been notified?"

"Julie has a brother and a mother who live in Boston," Stephanie said. "She and her husband were going through a divorce, but no one has been notified. This will break her mother's heart."

"I take it you were close to the decedent. Is that correct, Mrs. Rocco?"

"Yes."

The police chief turned to Rich and said, "I'd like you to start with how you happened to find her, and anything else you feel would be relevant to her death. I'm reluctant to call it murder at this point, although from what I saw, it certainly looked like she was murdered."

Rich told him about walking to her room to invite her for a celebratory glass of champagne and how he had found her. The police chief took notes and said, "Mrs. Rocco, she was your friend. What can you tell me about her?"

Mike was standing behind the police chief and Stephanie saw him slightly nod his head up and down, indicating she should tell the chief what she knew about Julie.

"Julie and I met in the doctorate program here at the university. We were both getting our degrees in Strategic Leadership with a concentration in Executive Coaching. We were both interested in physician leadership development. When we met she lived and worked in Boston, and I lived and worked in Portland, Oregon. Coincidentally, we both worked in the health care industry for a federally qualified health care center." She took the tissue Rich gave her and wiped away the tears that continued to trickle down her cheeks.

"I'm sorry to put you in this position, Mrs. Rocco, but I do need to find out everything I can related to the decedent. I hope you understand."

"I do. When she told me she and her husband were getting a divorce, I asked her if she would like to come to work for me in Portland. I'd been very impressed with her, and we'd become somewhat close friends. She took me up on my offer, moved to Portland, and started working for me at the company where I'm employed."

"How would you describe her relationship with her ex-husband?" the police chief asked.

"Well, for starters," Stephanie said, "he's not exactly her ex-husband. Their divorce won't be final until next month. From what Julie told me, it was simply a matter of growing apart. He owns a bed and breakfast in York, Maine, and she worked in Boston. She tried to go up there most weekends, but increasingly she found it difficult to manage her work, her studies, and her marriage. She once told me her marriage was what suffered the most. She never really said anything derogatory about him."

Her statement was interrupted by the sound of the chief's phone buzzing. He answered it and said, "You found the killer? Already? Who? Where?" Chief Anders listened and said, "I'll be there in a minute. See if the coroner can take both of them."

He turned to them and said, "Looks like we've found the killer. He had her wallet and what's probably her jewelry in his pocket along with what I'll bet is the murder weapon. I've got to go. I'll call you later and tell you what I find out. Mrs. Rocco, could you call the next of kin or would you like me to do it?"

"I'll take care of it. I've met her mother and as bad as it's going to be, it might help if a friend of Julie's broke the sad news to her."

The police chief was walking towards the door when Mike said, "Chief, if you don't mind, I'd like to come along and see what your deputies have found. Seems awfully convenient to find the killer that quick."

The chief whirled around and responded in a belligerent tone of voice, "Are you insinuating that we southerners might not take the necessary steps in solving a murder that you westerners do?"

"Not in the last bit, but you must admit, it sure makes it a lot easier when it happens that fast."

"Sometimes it just happens that way, Sheriff," he said sarcastically. "Sure, come on." Mike followed him out the door.

CHAPTER FOUR

"I am so dreading this call," Stephanie said, "but I guess there's nothing I can do to reverse what's happened. One way or another, her mother has to be told, and I'd rather she heard it from me than someone she's never met."

She took a deep breath, picked up her phone, and pressed in a number. A moment later she spoke into the phone and said, "Hello, this is Stephanie Rocco." She listened and then replied in a tense voice, "It's good to talk to you to, Celia. I need to talk to Mrs. Logan, but would you please do me a favor and stay near her while I talk to her? Unfortunately, I have some very bad news I have to tell her. Thanks, yes, please put her on." Stephanie looked pale, and she had a death grip on her phone as she waited for Mrs. Logan to come on the line.

"Hello, Mrs. Logan, it's Stephanie Rocco. Thank you, yes, we graduated, but I'm afraid I have some very bad news for you." She listened for a moment and then said, "It breaks my heart to tell you this, but Julie has been murdered. I don't know any details as of yet. I just finished speaking with the chief of police, and he told me his deputies have found the murderer. I'll call you when I know more. I am so, so sorry. Would you like me to call anyone for you?"

She listened for a moment. "You'll have Celia call your son and Julie's soon-to-be ex-husband? Thank you. I've not met either one of them. Here's my phone number if you need to call me. As soon as I find out any information about the murderer I'll let you know. Again, I am so sorry." She ended the call and sobbed deeply. Rich walked over to her and put his arms around her.

"Honey, there was nothing else you could do. She needed to be told and there's no way to sugarcoat a death message like the one you had to deliver. At least she has someone with her. I remember you telling me she was in bad health or something."

"Yes," Stephanie said through her tears. "She has stage four pancreatic cancer. Julie was going to fly up to Boston tomorrow to see her. She tried to visit her mother at least once a month. That poor woman. I can't even imagine what she must be feeling right now."

Just then Mike knocked on the door and opened it, a grim look on his face. "This is ridiculous," he said. "I've seen some sloppy police work in my time, but I think that chief of police just topped it."

"What are you talking about?" Kelly asked as the three of them looked at him expectantly.

"How convenient is it that a drunken transient bum, literally, is the person the chief of police is claiming committed the murder? Of course, he's dead, but that doesn't seem to matter. For the police chief it was an open and shut case. Now I suppose he can go back to doing whatever it is he was doing before he got the call and tie a big red ribbon around this investigation. According to him the crime has been solved, clean and simple."

"Why would he think a transient killed Stephanie?" Rich asked. "Why would she even come in contact with a person like that when she was safe in her room here at the hotel?"

"The chief's deputies found the bum lying behind a car in the parking lot. It looks like he died from a fractured skull suffered in a fall. He had Stephanie's wallet and jewelry in his pocket, and a pistol similar to the one he assumed killed Julie, just happened to be in his hand. I mean, how likely is it that a bum who's so drunk I doubt if he could stand up could go to her room, she'd open the door, he'd shoot her, and then take her personal effects?" Mike said angrily. "It's absurd to think that could happen. I simply can't accept it as being a reasonable explanation of how Julie was murdered." Clearly overwrought, Mike paced back and forth in the small room.

His pacing was interrupted by the sound of Stephanie's phone ringing. She looked at the monitor, sighed deeply and said, "It's Julie's mother."

"Hello, Mrs. Logan. I'd ask how you're doing, but I think I know the answer to that. Probably about as well as I am." She listened for a moment. "Yes, I can tell you what we know so far. A friend of mine who came to my graduation is married to a sheriff. He went with the chief of police when the chief got the call that the murderer had been found.

"The suspect was found dead lying in the hotel parking lot. The chief of police determined that Julie was killed by what appears to be a transient. Her jewelry and her wallet were found in his possession as well as the possible murder weapon. The chief believes he took a fall because he was drunk and hit his head on a concrete curb which caused his death. That's all we know at this point."

Stephanie listened for a few moments and then said, "No, I'm so sorry, but I can't come to Boston tomorrow. I have to get back to Oregon. I'm the keynote speaker at a large conference on Monday, and then my husband and I are leaving on a trip. Let me talk to the others. I'll get back to you in a few minutes."

She looked at Mike after she ended the call and said, "Mike, I think Mrs. Logan would agree with you. She asked me if I would fly to Boston tomorrow. She's certain Julie wasn't killed by a transient. When I told her I couldn't go to Boston, she asked if one of you would go there. She said she urgently needs to talk to someone and with her medical prognosis, she's not sure how much time she has left to live."

"Stephanie, under different circumstances I'd be happy to do that, but all heck has broken loose in Beaver County, and Kelly and I had to change our scheduled flight for tomorrow to an earlier time as it is. I have to meet with my chief deputy tomorrow afternoon as soon as I get back."

She turned to Kelly. "You've helped Mike solve several murder cases over the last few years. Would you go to Boston and at least talk to her? Rich could probably go, but he wouldn't know what to do with the information she said she has. I know this is a lot to ask, but if you're worried about the money, Mrs. Logan said she'd pay all the costs incurred in going to Boston. Please, Kelly, Julie was a wonderful person. She deserves more than to have her death go down as being killed by some transient, supposedly for her jewelry. I've never been involved in anything like this, but something doesn't smell right to me. I'd be curious to see what Mrs. Logan has to say."

"Kelly, I agree with Stephanie," Mike said. "You're very good at things like this, and I don't think you've ever been to Boston. It may just be the ramblings of an old woman, but on the other hand, she might have some insight as to who might have killed Julie. I have a real strong gut feeling it wasn't the transient. Anyway, you could use a couple more days off. The coffee shop practically runs itself with the help you have. What do you say?"

She looked at both of them and said, "I have no idea what I can do to help, but if nothing else, Mrs. Logan might get some closure on her daughter's death by talking to me. It might help her rest easier to tell someone whatever it is she wants to discuss. Okay, I guess I'm off to Boston."

"Thank you so much," Stephanie said. "I'll call her right now. You might as well go to your room and make your flight arrangements for Boston. I'll call you when I find out when she wants to meet with you. By the way, she lives in an incredible old Boston mansion. The trip will be worth it if just for that. Oh, one more thing. I'm cancelling the big celebratory dinner tonight. I'm not up to it. I'll call my family and tell them what's happened. I think a sandwich from room service will work just fine. Talk to you later."

"Wait a minute, Stephanie," Kelly said. "I have a question for you. When you called to tell us about her death, you said you knew it was going to happen, that it was in the stars. What did you mean?"

"You know I'm interested in astrology. I happened to look at Julie's chart before we came to Virginia, and it was very clear to me she was going to die. I know none of you probably believe me, but that's what I saw," Stephanie said twisting the Kleenex she was holding in her hands and looking away from them.

"I don't know what mumbo-jumbo that's all about, but I'm sure glad you didn't tell the police chief," Mike said. "He probably would have decided you needed to be committed to the local funny farm."

"Mike, don't," Kelly said. "Stephanie, I know you're a believer in astrology, but not everyone is. We can talk about this later, okay?"

"Okay."

CHAPTER FIVE

"Well," Kelly said as they entered their room, "I guess you never know what life's going to hand you. I don't know a thing about Boston other than there's a lot of history there. Actually, I've never been to the East Coast, so this whole trip is really unchartered territory for me."

"You know when you're traveling alone I like you to stay in a nice hotel," Mike said. "Anyway, I attended a conference once at The Parker House hotel in Boston. It wasn't cheap, but it was very safe, and since it's downtown it's within walking distance of a lot of historical places. I'll call and make a reservation there for you for tomorrow night and also the next night. After that, you'll have to see if you're coming home or what."

"Okay, while you're doing that I'll see when I can get a flight to Boston. I'll try to coordinate my departure time with when you're flying back to Portland. That way we can go to the airport together."

A few minutes later Mike looked over and saw that Kelly had ended her call. "Kelly, I was able to get you a reservation for two nights. Let's see what happens after that. By the way, the hotel is close to the airport, so you can take a cab when you get there. I'd rather you didn't try to drive while you're in Boston."

"Trust me, I have no desire to. I was able to get a flight to Boston an hour after you leave for Portland. We can return our rental car at the airport tomorrow morning, and that will work fine. You've got a ten o'clock flight and mine's at eleven."

"I think that's a good idea, and as I remember, parking is at a premium downtown. If you have time, think about taking The Old Time Trolley bus tour. I did it, and it really gave me an historic overview of the town. I think you'd enjoy it, and it's something you can tell your granddaughters about. They'll be studying it pretty soon if they haven't already," he said laughing.

When Mike married Kelly several years earlier he'd gained an instant family in the form of her daughter, Julia, and her son, Cash. When Julie, married Brad, a widower with two young daughters, Olivia and Ella, Mike's instant family became even larger. Having never had children, he loved every minute he spent with them, and as Kelly often pointed out to him, he'd become quite the doting grandfather.

Kelly picked up her ringing phone. "Kelly, it's Stephanie. I just spoke with Mrs. Logan, and she is so indebted to you for going up to Boston. She said she still attends church on Sundays, but she needs to rest after that. Monday morning, she has a chemotherapy treatment, so she'd like you to come to her home Monday afternoon. She said her driver would pick you up at your hotel at 1:00 Monday afternoon. Mrs. Logan said the car was a black Mercedes limousine. I'm to text her with the name of your hotel when you have one."

"That's fine. I'll be staying at The Parker House. I guess it's kind of an institution in Boston, so her driver will probably know where it is. Would you text her telephone number to me in case there's a problem?"

"Will do, and Kelly, you'll never know how much I appreciate this."

"I have no idea if I can help or even how I can help, but something does seem off to me. I'm also sorry your special graduation day turned out to be so bad. You've worked so hard to get here. It's a darn shame it has to end this way."

"Yes, but who knows? Maybe this is why you said you'd come to my graduation. Maybe you were supposed to solve a murder."

"I think that's a stretch. Tell your family good-bye for us, and again, Stephanie, congratulations. We're going to follow your lead and get a sandwich from room service for dinner. We need to pack and make some calls. I'll let you know what Mrs. Logan has to say."

After she ended the call, Kelly turned to Mike and said, "I'm emotionally beat. I really would like to have room service for dinner. Is that okay with you?"

"I assume you'll have your usual comfort food sandwich of pastrami and Swiss cheese on rye with French fries and a dill pickle," he said shaking his head.

"Yup, been a tough day. That sounds wonderful."

"It may sound wonderful, but I don't think it's normal."

"Quite frankly," Kelly said, "I think normal is highly overrated!"

"As if you'd know, sweetheart, as if you'd know."

CHAPTER SIX

Kelly and Mike turned their rental car in at the airport and walked the short distance to security. Fortunately, the line wasn't long and when they'd passed through it, Mike said, "Great, we've got an hour before my plane takes off. Let's get some breakfast. I've got a long flight ahead of me, and I better load up on some food now, because I know the only thing I'll be getting on the plane is some stale pretzels."

After they finished breakfast they walked to Mike's departure gate and saw that his plane was just starting to board. The large middle-aged sheriff put his arms around Kelly and said, "Be careful. I know I don't need to tell you this, but if the itinerant guy wasn't the murderer, that means the killer is still at large. Don't take any chances. You're staying in a very safe hotel, but ultimately, you're responsible for your own safety. Keep your door locked and watch your back. I wish I could be with you, but I really do need to get back." He took her face in his hands and kissed her. "I love you, Kelly. See you in a couple of days." He walked to where the gate agent was collecting the passengers' boarding passes, turned and waved to her, and then walked down the jet way to the waiting plane.

Kelly walked over to a nearby large television monitor and found her flight information. She was glad the airport wasn't all that large, because her flight was leaving from a gate at the other end of the terminal from where Mike's had been. She leisurely walked to her gate, sat down, and read the newspaper she'd bought. Before she knew it, her flight was being announced, and she was soon on her way to Boston.

*****

Because she'd planned on being in Virginia only for the weekend, Kelly had packed lightly. She easily retrieved her small roller bag from the baggage carousel and walked out to the taxi line. "The Parker House," she said to the taxi driver. Moments later she was in a long tunnel and it seemed to her like every other car on the East Coast was in there as well.

I'm so glad they don't have tunnels like this in Cedar Bay. I feel claustrophobic just thinking about them, much less being in one. At least they don't have earthquakes here, or I'd seriously be worrying about whether I'm going to make it out at the other end.

"Here you are, ma'am," the taxi driver said as he pulled up to the curb in front of the hotel. Her door was immediately opened by a valet, and her bag was put on a luggage cart. She paid the driver and walked through the lobby to the registration desk. Moments later, electronic room key in hand, she followed the porter into the elevator and up to her room. He opened the door and put her bag on the luggage rack at the foot of the bed.

"May I bring you some ice or get you anything else?" the young man asked.

"No thanks," Kelly said as she tipped him. "How is the restaurant downstairs?"

"If you're talking about Parker's Restaurant, it's great. Guests tell me that all the time. Boston cream pie and Parker House rolls were both created here. You might as well try them while you're here. If you like Italian food, there's a street in the North End named Hanover Street, that's just one Italian restaurant after another. I've never heard anyone complain about a meal they had there."

"Thanks, I might try it tomorrow night. For now, I think I'll unpack, and then I'll probably take a walk and orient myself."

"One more thing," he said. "If you're only going to be here a couple of days, you might want to take a bus tour. You can go to the concierge downstairs, and they can buy a ticket for you online. It really gives you a nice overview of the city and its history."

"Thank you very much. You've been very helpful."

After he'd left she looked around the room, pleased with Mike's choice. The hotel was definitely downtown and close to the airport. The ride from the airport had only taken a few minutes, even with the tunnel experience.

She looked at her watch and realized Mike hadn't even arrived in Portland, and he still had to drive to Cedar Bay once he got there. A welcoming letter on the desk caught her eye, and she read that the hotel, which dated from 1855, was located along the Freedom Trail and close to Beacon Hill, Boston Common, Quincy Market, and the Faneuil Hall marketplace. Although some of the names rang a bell with her from high school history classes she'd taken long ago, she decided she'd never find them on her own. The fact that both Mike and the porter had recommended the bus tour made her decide to make a reservation when she went downstairs. Since she wasn't meeting Mrs. Logan until early tomorrow afternoon, she could easily fit the bus tour in during the morning.

CHAPTER SEVEN

Kelly opened one eye and looked at the clock on the nightstand. It was seven in the morning. Her full stomach sent a message to her brain that it could have done without the third Parker House roll and the Boston cream pie she had for dessert the night before. She ignored it and chalked it up to research. She was determined to learn how to make the cream pie, and if she could, it would be a great addition to her menu at Kelly's Koffee Shop.

Thankful the room was equipped with a coffee pot, she made herself a cup and took it into the bathroom while she got ready for the day. During her walk after she'd checked into the hotel yesterday, she'd noticed a bagel shop across the street from the hotel and down a block. Even though she was still full from the dinner she had the evening before, a bagel and a second cup of coffee sounded like a great way to start the day. She'd gotten the tour bus ticket yesterday and could use it anytime today, getting off and back on the bus at as many places as she wanted to.

Fortified with coffee and a bagel, she boarded the tour bus and was pleasantly surprised at the comfortable seating. Two hours later she felt she knew far more about Boston than she had when she'd studied it in school all those years ago. Names and events from the past like Paul Revere, Samuel Adams, and The Boston Tea Party, had come alive for her. She saw where the tea had been dumped into the harbor by the Sons of Liberty and also saw the Old North Church where the signal light in the church steeple sent Paul Revere off on his midnight ride into history. As soon as the tour guide pointed out the church, the words from the famous Longfellow poem kept playing themselves over and over in her mind, as if they were on a never-ending loop. "One if by land, two if by sea," was the signal used to guide the midnight ride of Paul Revere on the eve of the American Revolutionary War.

At the conclusion of the tour she stepped off the bus and walked back to the hotel, her head swimming with all she'd seen from the North End to the Boston Common. Kelly was sorry Mike hadn't been with her to see Fenway Park, the baseball stadium that's home to the Boston Red Sox. He'd often talked about the stadium and what a part of sports history it was. She hoped it had been on the tour he'd taken. Her bus tour had taken her to the North End, and she'd seen Hanover Street, the street the porter said had so many wonderful Italian restaurants. The tour guide had raved about the restaurants there.

Without even bothering to go into the hotel and freshen up she told the doorman to call a taxi, because she wanted to go to Hanover Street for lunch. Within minutes the cab driver pulled over to the curb to pick her up and a few minutes later when he stopped on Hanover Street, she could smell the Italian food. Her mouth began to water in anticipation.

She walked along the street for several blocks, looking in the restaurant windows, and finally decided on one called Panza. Kelly knew it sounded silly, but for some reason it reminded her of the trip she and Mike had taken to Tuscany. She laughed to herself remembering how excited they had been about attending a five day cooking school in Tuscany, never dreaming they'd end up solving a murder while they were there.

As she opened the door a young waiter greeted her. "Welcome, *signora*. Just one for lunch?"

"Yes."

"Ahh, that is too bad. A woman as beautiful as you should never dine alone, but please follow me, and I will seat you at the best table in the house, only the best for a woman such as you."

Now that definitely reminds me of Italy. I think this will be a very authentic experience, she thought, smiling at the young man.

He handed her a menu and she immediately spotted a dish named *Linguine Alla Pescatore* which jumped off the page and commanded her attention. She read that it was the signature dish of the house with scallops, mussels, shrimp, octopus, and clams in a traditional *Fra Diavolo* sauce served over linguine. She remembered from her trip to Italy that *Fra Diavolo* meant "brother devil" and was a delightful spicy tomato sauce. It sounded wonderful.

"That was fast, *signora*. You have chosen?" the young waiter with the impossibly long black eyelashes asked.

"Yes. Here's what I want," she said pointing to the menu with her finger. "I'd try to say it, but I could never do it justice. Thank you." She looked around the small intimate restaurant and decided she'd chosen well, and since there wasn't an empty table she assumed it was a very popular restaurant. She felt lucky to get a table, and the best in the house at that according to her waiter. She noticed a line had begun to form outside the door, another good sign she'd chosen well.

A few minutes later the waiter brought her dish, and she spent a moment looking at it, savoring it with her mind before her mouth began to taste it. She knew this was one dish that would definitely not be on the menu at Kelly's Koffee Shop. It needed to be prepared right before serving, and that wouldn't work at her coffee shop.

Enjoying every bite of it, she finished and sat back, wondering how the person who had been so full when she'd gotten up that morning had managed to consume an entire plate of seafood and pasta only a few hours later.

If I'd walked around the city I could justify eating it, but sitting in a bus and never moving for two hours hardly qualifies. Oh well, no regrets. It was wonderful, she thought.

After she'd paid the bill, she stepped out onto the sidewalk and saw a cab in front of the restaurant. Within minutes the driver had taken her back to the hotel so she could get ready for her meeting with Mrs. Logan. She had no idea what to expect, but thought she better take a pen and some paper with her in case she needed to take notes.

Notes are handy to have, but when the information leads to a hunt for a killer, they're of little value.

CHAPTER EIGHT

Promptly at 1:00 that afternoon a black Mercedes limousine pulled up in front of the hotel. The driver, dressed in a black suit, got out and walked around the car, opening the back door. Kelly walked towards him and said, "I'm assuming you're Mrs. Logan's driver?"

"Yes, Mrs. Reynolds. My name is Jasper. Please, make yourself comfortable. It's a short drive, but since it's a warm day, I put a bottle of water next to your seat." After securing her door he walked around the car, got in, and pulled away from the curb. "Please let me know if you're comfortable. If not, I can make the temperature warmer or cooler for you."

"Thank you, Jasper. It's just fine. I've not met Mrs. Logan before. Can you tell me a little about her?"

"I've been Mrs. Logan's driver for coming up on twenty years. She's a wonderful person. The last year has been very hard for her. I'm sure you know she's in ill health. She never complains, but I'm certain she's in a great deal of pain. I wish there was something I could do to help her. The staff loves her."

"How many people does she have on her staff?" Kelly asked, thinking this must be a wealthy person if she could afford to have a staff.

"Well, let's see. There's Celia. She's Mrs. Logan's caregiver and is always with her. Before that she was her secretary. You'll be meeting her today. I won't bother you with the names of the rest of the staff, but there is a gardener, two maids, and a cook. Of course there are other people who do things like clean the windows, paint, etcetera. The staff are the ones who work for her full-time."

"Thank you. You said she has two maids. From that I'm assuming she lives in a large home."

"Oh, yes. It's a beautiful old home on Bunker Hill. It's been in her husband's family for generations. When he died she stayed in it even though it's way too much house for her. I don't know what will happen to it now that Miss Julie's dead. I think Mrs. Logan always hoped she'd move back here and live in it. I'd hate to see it torn down so condominiums could be built on the site, although real estate on Bunker Hill is very expensive and at a real premium, so I suppose that could happen.

"Her son lives here in Boston, but between you and me, I don't think he could afford to live in the house and keep it up. Last I heard he wasn't working, and I probably shouldn't say this, but the word is that Mrs. Logan supports him. There's her house, the five story brick one. I'll let you out here, open the gate for you, and then I'll park in back."

Kelly stepped out of the limousine and looked up at the imposing five story late 19th century house, finding it hard to believe that only one person lived in it, not counting the staff. It looked like it could easily accommodate several families.

Jasper unlatched the gate for her. Beyond it was an expanse of green grass that ended in a hedge at the house. She walked up the three broad steps leading to the large mahogany encased leaded glass doors. Enormous terra cotta planters on either side of the door had brightly colored petunias spilling out of them. Jasper knocked on the door and then walked back to the limousine.

A moment later the front door was opened by a woman who

appeared to be in her fifties. Her grey hair was pulled back into a bun, accentuating the smooth light coffee color of her skin. She wore a simple white cotton blouse tucked into black pants. She put her hand out and said, "Mrs. Reynolds, I'm Celia. Welcome to the Logan House. Please come in. Mrs. Logan is in the drawing room."

Kelly stood for a moment trying to let what she was seeing with her eyes register with her brain. The natural light-filled home was simply magnificent with its big rooms, wide staircase, high ceilings, and floor-to-ceiling windows. The wide curving staircase in front of her reminded her of something out of Gone with the Wind.

She followed Celia into the drawing room which had textured walls covered in warm tan-colored grass cloth. At the far end of the room was a fireplace with a marble mantel flanked by tall windows with shutters. Everywhere she looked there was a feeling of gracious elegance.

Celia walked towards two wingback chairs upholstered in a tan and white plaid with yellow accents. In one of them sat a small grey-haired woman with a blanket covering her legs. Even though she'd become small with age and illness, when she smiled she appeared to be the young vibrant woman she once must have been. "Mrs. Reynolds, I'm Marcy Logan. Please, sit down," she said, gesturing towards the other wingback chair. "I want to thank you for coming on such short notice. Celia will bring us some iced tea. It's rather warm today, and I think that's a much better choice than coffee, don't you?"

"Yes, thank you. That sounds quite refreshing. I want you to know how sorry I am to meet you under these circumstances. No mother should outlive her child, and for a child to die in the manner that Julie did is a tragedy. If there is anything I can do to help, let me know, and please call me Kelly."

"Kelly, I don't know how much Stephanie told you about me. Let me give you a little background before I tell you why I asked you to come here. I have stage four pancreatic cancer. The doctors, and believe me, I've seen the best, give me only a few more months at best to live unless a miracle takes place. The chemotherapy, horrible as it is, has bought me a little time.

"As you can see from this house, I not only can afford the best doctors in the world, I can also afford the best people to find out who murdered my daughter. I could interview people for weeks to find the perfect one, but I'm not sure how many weeks I have left. That's why I want to hire you to find the murderer. I will pay you well. Stephanie speaks very highly of you and told me you were helpful in solving a couple of murders. We need to get started immediately." With that she sat back in her chair, seemingly exhausted by the vehemence of her speech.

"Mrs. Logan, I'm flattered you would want me to help you, but I must be honest with you. I'm not a professional private investigator. My husband is the sheriff in Beaver County, Oregon, and although I've helped him solve several murder cases, I'm sure a lot of it was due to luck. Fortunately, my husband inherited quite a bit of money from his aunt, so I wouldn't take any money from you even if I did accept your offer."

"Kelly, I'm not used to having anyone say no to me, and at this stage of my life, I'm certainly not going to settle for no. I liked you the minute I saw you, and I didn't get to where I am by not trusting my instincts. Even though my husband was born into a Boston family that was wealthy and well-known, he founded and owned a large insurance company. While I never worked in his company, I was very involved in every aspect of it from my office here at home He often said I was the reason it was so successful. He was the type of person that wavered over difficult business decisions, but I didn't. For whatever reason we were a great good cop, bad cop pair, or so I believe that's the term used these days. Even if you won't accept my money, we need to get started."

"Mrs. Logan, I don't recall saying yes."

"You didn't outwardly, but inside I think you did. Maybe you don't need the money, but I'll pay all of your costs. As I said, I don't have any time to waste. The first thing you need to know is that I transferred ten million dollars into my daughter's checking account last week. I gave it to her as a graduation present."

Kelly sat for a moment, somewhat stunned by this revelation and also very much aware that ten million dollars could provide a very large motive for why Julie Jensen was murdered.

CHAPTER NINE

"Mrs. Logan, I've never heard of anyone being able to transfer that large of an amount with a wire transfer. I'm sure the manager of Julie's bank must have put a hold on it. Actually, maybe there's still a hold on it," Kelly said.

"Under ordinary circumstances, that would be correct, but this was not an ordinary circumstance. My banker is a very good friend of mine, and he personally called the manager of Julie's bank to let him know that the transfer was legitimate. Within minutes, the money was in Julie's account with no hold placed on it. When the transaction had been completed, I called her and told her what I'd done, and please don't call me Mrs. Logan. From now on you can call me Marcy."

"All right, Marcy," Kelly said. "A number of things come to mind, the first being, and trust me, I know next to nothing about tax laws, but isn't there something about you having to pay a large amount of taxes on that transfer because it's a gift? Wouldn't you have saved a lot of tax money if you'd willed it to her instead? I'm sorry, but you said you don't know how much time you have left, and if that's true, why did you give it to her now and get stuck with having to pay a gift tax?"

"That's a very good question, and I asked my attorney about it. Actually I would have had to pay taxes on anything over five million dollars whether it was a gift during my lifetime or whether she received that amount from my estate after I died.

"The reason I did it is I wanted to be alive when Julie received it. She was supposed to inherit almost everything else of mine when I die, including this house, but I wanted to be able to see her do something for herself. She's worked so hard to get to where she is, and since she was in the process of dissolving her marriage, I hoped the ten million dollar gift would give her the financial freedom to do whatever she wanted, like maybe take a long trip. I wanted Julie to do something just for Julie."

"Of course that brings us to the question of who knew she'd received the money," Kelly said. "From what the police chief said at the hotel, the transient had her jewelry and her wallet, but there was only about one hundred and fifty dollars in it. Doesn't sound like she was murdered for her money."

"No, I think you're right, but that was what I thought when Stephanie first told me about the details of her murder."

"So," Kelly said, "in that case, I guess the next thing would be to try and figure out who would get that money if Julie died, assuming of course, they even knew she'd received such a generous gift from you."

"Yes, that's what I've been thinking as well. I suppose the obvious person to look to when there's that kind of money involved is Julie's brother, my son, Clint Logan. He and Julie weren't close, so I rather doubt she'd tell him I'd given her the money, particularly knowing it would infuriate him."

"What can you tell me about your son?"

Mrs. Logan clasped her hands together and twisted them tightly in front of her, clearly agitated. Celia walked over and put a reassuring hand on her shoulder and said, "Marcy, you don't have to do this. Maybe you should rest for a while and continue this discussion at some other time."

"Celia, we both know I don't have much time left. In my case, it's got to be done now or never. I'm okay." She continued to speak,

"My son has not had a particularly happy life. He's been divorced three times and has never had children. I never did feel any of his three wives were right for him, but he was dazzled by their looks. I think all of them just wanted the money they thought he had." Celia poured Marcy a glass of water from a cut glass pitcher that reflected the sunlight streaming into the room, casting a rainbow prism of color on the far wall of the room.

"Did your son join your husband's insurance company?" Kelly asked, trying to get a better sense of Julie's brother.

"Yes, very briefly, but it was not a very good experience," Marcy said as a shadow passed over her face. "Clint felt since he was the son of the owner he should be made vice-president when he joined the company. My husband felt that title had to be earned and told Clint when he'd sold enough insurance, he'd promote him to the title of manager, and he would have. He was essentially saying Clint had to prove himself. It infuriated Clint, and he stormed out of my husband's office and never returned. It almost broke my husband's heart, but both he and Clint were stubborn."

"Since he didn't go into the family business, what type of business is he in?" Kelly asked.

Marcy looked down at her hands again and then up at Kelly. "At the moment he isn't working," she said quietly. She took a deep breath and added, "I'm supporting him."

"I see," Kelly said.

"Actually, it's probably all my fault. He's seven years younger than Julie, and they were never close. She excelled at everything she did, and it was so hard for me to see him living in her shadow and never measuring up to what she accomplished. I admit I spoiled him and shielded him, or at least that's what my husband said. We had many arguments over the situation with Clint, but as a mother, I didn't want to see him hurt. In retrospect, I wish I'd acted differently. It's pretty sad when a man is thirty-nine years old, has never really held a job, has three failed marriages, and his mother supports him. I'm sure some people would say it's pretty pathetic."

"Being a parent is never easy," Kelly said. "I have two children, so I understand what you're saying. As for Clint, did you and he ever discuss what you intended to do with your wealth?"

"He saw an envelope on my desk from my lawyer last week and asked me if I'd decided what I was going to do with my estate. I told him I'd come to a decision, and he would be taken care of. I did not tell him I was giving the money to Julie."

"Marcy, I'm sorry, but I have to ask this question. If Clint thought you were getting ready to do something with your money, and he was afraid he was going to get a much smaller amount than he'd been counting on, do you think he could be capable of murder?"

"No, absolutely not," she said slapping her hand on the arm of her chair. "Clint is a lot of things, or not a lot of things, but however you want to look at it, he is not a murderer. That I'm certain of. The most I could ever see him do is tell his sister that he should be entitled to half of it, hope she'd agree with him, and give it to him."

"All right, and I'm really not trying to make this painful for you, but as I told you, my husband is a sheriff, and over the years I've seen him look primarily at one thing when he's trying to solve a murder. Who has the most to gain when someone is murdered? In this case it seems like your son would have a lot to gain. There's also the thought that with Julie being deceased and no longer being an heir, he would be entitled to receive the full one hundred percent of your estate rather than fifty percent. I know that's not a pretty thought, but if I'm going to help you, we need to be honest with each other."

Marcy's piercing blue eyes looked directly into Kelly's and she said in a steely voice, "You must believe me when I tell you Clint had nothing to do with this. That subject is closed. I do think we need to look at Julie's ex-husband or whatever you call a husband when the divorce hasn't been finalized."

"Please, tell me about him."

"His name is Mark Jensen, and I think he had a very good motive for murdering Julie."

CHAPTER TEN

"Why do you think Julie's husband, who wasn't quite an ex at the time of her murder, had a good motive for killing her?" Kelly asked.

"His business is on the verge of bankruptcy," Marcy said taking another sip of water from the glass Celia held for her.

"What kind of business is it? Tell me about him. How did they meet? What's he like?"

"Mark owns a bed and breakfast in York, Maine. Someone told Julie about it several years ago, and she decided she needed to take a few days off from work and just relax. She spent a week at the bed and breakfast, and that's how they met. It was before she started her doctoral program. She fell in love with him and a few months later they were married. His family has lived in Maine for one hundred and fifty years or more, and the bed and breakfast has been the primary source of income for the family for the past century or so.

"It consists of a main house and several cottages located on a bluff overlooking the Atlantic. There is also a very good restaurant on the premises. There are plenty of authentic antiques in the house and cottages, and they've been through a number of renovations as the guests demanded the latest modern accommodations. The last renovation occurred just after Julie started her doctoral program. Mark was supposed to recoup the money it cost for the upgrades within one season, and believe me, the seasons are short that far north. Anyway, there was a downturn in the economy and visits to bed and breakfasts in Maine weren't a high priority when people were being laid off work, gas prices had gone through the roof, and the future for a lot of people was pretty uncertain. In fact, business became so bad Mark mentioned several times he might have to declare bankruptcy."

"How did Julie deal with it? Was she ever involved in it?" Kelly asked.

"No, she'd worked her way up the corporate ladder to the position of vice-president of the health care company she'd been with for many years. She and Mark decided they would have an unconventional marriage, one in which he spent the summers in Maine, as well as a couple of months beforehand getting ready for the season, and a couple of months after the season had ended, taking care of winterizing everything. They spent some time together in Boston, but with Mark gone for so many months, Julie had a lot of spare time on her hands. She and Mark made a decision not to have children because of their living arrangement. That's when she decided to get involved in the doctoral program."

"I agree that a looming bankruptcy provides a motive for murder, but since they were getting divorced, he wouldn't be entitled to any of her money. I'm assuming if she had a will she'd changed it, so that he wouldn't get anything upon her death," Kelly said.

"In an ideal world that would be true. Unfortunately, few of us live in an ideal world, and Julie certainly didn't. The last time I talked to Julie, right after I told her about the ten million dollars, I asked her if she had changed her will. She told me she was going to do it as soon as she returned from Virginia. One of the things that causes me a great deal of concern is that Mark might still be in her will."

"I can certainly understand your concern, but a couple of things come to mind. First of all, do you think he knew she hadn't changed her will?"

"I have no idea," Marcy said. "It was an amicable divorce, actually Mark didn't want the divorce and told Julie he still loved her. She felt the marriage had become one in name only and that maybe she could find someone in Portland with whom she could have a meaningful relationship. At least I think that's the term they're using these days."

"All right, so we really have no way of knowing whether or not he was in her will. Do you know the name of her attorney?"

"I don't. Like so many children of wealthy parents, Julie wanted to have her own attorney. I know she had one in Portland, because she told me that although he was her attorney, he wasn't licensed in Massachusetts, and a lawyer here in Boston was actually handling the divorce."

"I think when I return to Oregon, I'll go to her home and see if I can find her attorney's business card or his name."

"Since the divorce papers were filed here in Massachusetts, I would think you could find out the name of the attorney who's taking care of it, and maybe he would tell you the name of her attorney in Portland."

"Marcy, that's an excellent idea. Now one last question about Mark."

"Okay, but I can feel myself wearing down. There's one more suspect I want to talk to you about, but what did you want to know about Mark?"

"Do you think there's any way Mark would know about Julie receiving the ten million dollars from you?"

"I don't know. I don't see her casually calling him up and telling him, I mean that's not something people do, particularly to your soon to be ex-husband. She could have talked to him, and it might have slipped out, but I was under the impression she'd washed her hands of him, and they weren't in contact. I could be wrong."

"When I leave here, I'll see if I can find out who was representing her in her divorce case here in Massachusetts. Now, I think you mentioned you have one more suspect in mind."

"Yes, my granddaughter."

"What?" Kelly exclaimed as she inadvertently stood up and stared at Marcy with a look of both surprise and disbelief on her face. "No one ever told me Julie had a daughter. Stephanie certainly never mentioned it."

CHAPTER ELEVEN

"Marcy, are you sure you're strong enough to continue with this?" Celia asked, a worried look on her face.

"Yes. If Kelly's going to find out who murdered Julie, she has to know everything." She turned to Kelly. "This is not a pretty story, but probably a common one. Julie was near the end of her senior year in high school when she became pregnant. She was smart enough to know that the father of the child would not be good husband material, and being Catholic, she was very opposed to abortion, so she went to Pennsylvania to stay with my sister during her pregnancy. She had a baby girl whose name is Megan Simmons. Actually, I'll never forget the day she gave birth to her daughter. It was on October 20th. Anyway, she gave the baby up for adoption in Pennsylvania, and returned here to attend Harvard. Since Harvard's only five miles away from our home here on Bunker Hill, she lived here."

"How did your husband handle the news of her pregnancy?" Kelly asked.

"Not well. He was furious. He adored Julie and was sure the young man had taken advantage of her. He threatened to go to the young man's parents and make him pay for everything. Julie refused to name the father, and wouldn't allow any of us to be with her when she had the baby. She signed the consent to adopt papers while she was in the hospital and essentially gave up her daughter."

"That must have been a very difficult time for all of you."

"Trust me, you have no idea. I don't think my husband ever quite recovered from it. He was never the same. He had a major heart attack several years later and died soon after that. Privately, I've always thought the shock of his daughter having a child out of wedlock ate at him and eventually caused the heart attack."

"What was it like with Julie living here while she attended Harvard? I would think it would have put a strain on the family."

"Julie was the one who suggested she live with us while she attended Harvard. She did have one firm request. None of us were to mention the child she'd given up for adoption. I never did and to my knowledge my husband and Clint didn't either."

"All right, that gives me the background on the child Julie gave up for adoption, but I don't see what that has to do with her murder."

"Marcy," Celia interrupted, "I really think you need to rest. This has been too exhausting for you, and I'm starting to get concerned. I recognize the signs. I know the doctor gave you that new experimental drug last week, but even if it works, you shouldn't be going through this type of emotional turmoil."

"I promise I'll rest within the hour. I need to finish this. Kelly, when I spoke with Julie last week she told me she knew I wasn't going to be happy about it, but she'd met with her daughter. The only thing we knew about the birth was that it was a girl."

"How did her daughter find Julie?" Kelly asked. "I thought adoption records were sealed and only in rare cases, and only if both the child and the biological parent agreed, could they be opened."

"Yes," Marcy said. "What you say is true, however, in Pennsylvania, where Julie had her baby, as well as in a couple of other states, there is a provision that adopted children may have access to the medical history of their biological parents. When Julie gave her up for adoption, she submitted her family medical history with the adoption records, in case her daughter had a medical condition which would require that she know the family medical history."

"Okay, but I still don't see how the child, or I guess young woman, found Julie. I can understand her obtaining the family's medical history, but how was she able to find Julie?"

"I asked Julie the same thing, and she told me her daughter is not only a beautiful redhead, she's also as smart as Julie. She went to law school in San Francisco and specialized in family law. Possibly because she was given up for adoption, she's become an expert in that area of law. Her daughter told her that once she realized she could obtain the medical records of the family, with a little bribery, she was also able to find out that Julie was her mother and also her address at the time of her birth.

"Julie had used our home address here in Boston rather than my sister's Pennsylvania address. She found Julie on the Internet. She was also able to get her phone number, and she called her. I don't know how she did that, but I suppose with computers you can find anyone."

"All I can say is wow! How did Julie feel about it?"

"She'd felt guilty for all those years about giving up her daughter, so she was thrilled to finally have the chance to connect with her. Several times in the last few years she mentioned she wished she'd raised her as a single parent, since it's quite socially acceptable to do so these days."

"Marcy, what makes you think your granddaughter murdered Julie?"

"It was a passing comment by Julie, but it's stayed with me, particularly in light of the events that have occurred. She told Julie she'd like to meet her grandmother which of course is me. Through Julie, and using the Internet, I'm sure she found out about our family and the fact that her grandmother is quite wealthy."

"That's quite possible, but why would she murder Julie after she was just reunited with her?"

"I don't know. Possibly anger at having been given up for adoption," Marcy said. "Julie told me she'd lived in a number of different foster homes, and her childhood had not been a happy one. Evidently she was able to go to college and law school on scholarships. That's really all I know about her."

"Why did she say she needed to see her medical records?"

"She told Julie she'd made up a story about having a history of mental illness issues, and the person she talked to believed her. She also said she'd forged some medical records to prove it."

"So what I hear you saying is what if she resented Julie all the time she was growing up because she gave Megan up for adoption and then later she discovers her biological grandmother is very wealthy. It wouldn't be much of a stretch for her to think about what would happen if her mother was no longer around, and she could prove she was a legal heir to her grandmother's fortune. Maybe Megan wasn't kidding when she claimed she had some mental issues," Kelly said.

"Marcy, as your caregiver I'm going to overrule you. You need to rest, and you need to do it right now. Let me help you get up." Celia turned to Kelly. "It will take me a few minutes to get Marcy upstairs, and then I'll tell Jasper to take you back to your hotel."

"Give me one more minute, Celia," Marcy said as she put her hand on Kelly's arm. "Thank you so much for agreeing to help. I think you need to go to York and talk to Mark. After that it would probably be a good idea to see what you can find in Julie's home out in Portland. As for Megan, I think you need to find out more about her. Celia will call you later with Mark's information. You can rent a car and drive there. It's not far, only about a hundred miles."

She turned and Celia supported her as they slowly walked to the elevator on the far side of the room. A moment later Kelly heard the whir of the elevator as it rose to the third floor where Marcy's bedroom was located.

I've got to run this by Mike. I really need some advice. I certainly wasn't planning on extending my stay here and going to York, but I have to admit, this is a fascinating case. I wonder if Roxie would be willing to run the coffee shop for me for the rest of the week. That would give me enough time to drive to York, interview Mark, spend the night, and come back here to Boston to catch a flight back to the West Coast.

Since I have to fly into Portland anyway, I might as well check out Julie's house. If I find something there about her daughter, I might have to make a trip to San Francisco where Julie told Marcy that Megan lives. Although I wasn't planning on it, I guess I'm already involved. Think there's an old saying that goes, "In for a penny, in for a pound." It's kind of like the modern day version of "I'm all in."

A few moments later Kelly heard the whir of the elevator as it returned from Marcy's floor. The door opened and Celia walked out. "I'm sorry I felt I had to end the conversation, but I could tell Marcy was at the end of her strength. She needs to rest for several hours."

"She's a lovely lady, and very lucky to have someone like you to care for her," Kelly said.

"Thank you, but it's me who's the lucky one. She's the most wonderful person I've ever met. I don't think there's a non-profit organization in Boston that hasn't benefited from her generosity. I've worked for Marcy for most of my adult years. I started out as her secretary, and then when she was diagnosed with cancer several years ago I became her caregiver. Thank you for meeting with her. No one should have to go through what she's going through right now."

"I agree, and I guess I'll be helping her as well. You said something earlier about an experimental drug. What was that all about?"

"Marcy has a very fine doctor, and he thinks a drug that was just discovered may help her. It's terribly expensive. As a matter of fact, very few people have been able to afford it, so not much is known about it. He feels there's a good chance it will shrink the tumor, and she will be able to live several more years pain free. In other words, the cancer will go into remission for what could be a long time."

"That would be wonderful," Kelly said. "When will you know if it's working?"

"She's scheduled to have blood work done next week, and that should give us some idea if it's been effective. The one thing he did tell her was that she was not to get overly tired. That's the reason I was so adamant earlier. I'll call you later with the information about Mark." She picked up the house phone and pressed a button. "Jasper, Mrs. Reynolds is ready to return to her hotel."

She hung up the phone and said, "He'll meet you in front of the house in a few minutes. Again, thanks for coming. As tired as Marcy is, I think this has given her hope that someone will try and find her daughter's murderer, and she can get some type of closure to this tragedy. I'll talk to you later." She walked back to the elevator and once again Kelly heard the whir of the machinery as it took her up to Marcy's room.

A maid who had been standing by the front door opened it for Kelly and said, "Good day, ma'am."

Kelly settled into the back seat of the limousine and after Jasper got in behind the wheel she said, "Jasper, could you take me to the county courthouse? It has to do with my meeting with Mrs. Logan. I don't think it will take me very long."

"Not a problem. It's very close by. There's no parking at the courthouse, so I'll just keep circling until you come out, if that's okay with you."

"That's fine. Thank you."

A short time later he pulled into the loading zone in front of the courthouse. "We're here, let me come around and let you out."

"Thanks, but as busy as these streets are, I think you're better off staying where you are. I'm perfectly capable of letting myself out. See you in a few minutes."

As soon as she walked through the courthouse door she saw a guard and walked up to him. "Could you direct me to the family law clerk's office?" she asked.

"Certainly, in fact, I can do better than that." He took a map out of his pocket and circled where the office was, circled where she was standing, drew a line between the two circles, and handed her the map.

"Thank you so much. I really appreciate it."

"Not a problem. We're here to help," he said giving her a mock salute.

A few minutes later she walked up to a clerk seated behind a long counter. "I'd like to know who the attorney of record is for the wife in a certain divorce case. Can you help me?" Kelly asked.

"Certainly. What's the name of the case?"

"The two people getting divorced are Julie and Mark Jensen. That's really all I know."

"As long as you have the last name, it shouldn't be a problem." She spent a few minutes looking at her computer monitor and then said, "The attorney is Sean O'Brien. He does a lot of divorce cases here."

"Thank you. Does it give his telephone number on whatever you're looking at?"

"Sure does. I'll write it down for you. You might be able to reach him at his office. The family law judge came down sick this morning and had to cancel the cases that were on her docket this afternoon. Seems like I saw Sean's name on the list of cases that were cancelled. Here's his number and good luck!" She handed Kelly a piece of paper with the attorney's name and telephone number on it.

"Thank you so much. You've really been helpful, and I appreciate it."

"My pleasure," the clerk said turning back to her computer monitor.

A few minutes later Kelly spotted the black limousine slowly coming down the street. She waved to get Jasper's attention and walked to the curb. When he pulled up she had to walk between two cars stopped in the traffic lane to get into the limousine. He hadn't been joking. Parking was a really problem.

"Shall I take you to the hotel, Mrs. Reynolds?"

"Yes, please."

CHAPTER TWELVE

"Thanks, Jasper, I appreciate the ride and the detour to the courthouse," Kelly said as he held the door of the limousine open for her.

"It's been a pleasure talking to you, Mrs. Reynolds. I hope to see you again." The large black Mercedes limousine quietly slipped back into the flow of traffic, and Kelly walked through the hotel door the valet was holding open for her. A few minutes later she unlocked the door of her room, realizing how tired the conversation with Mrs. Logan had made her.

If I'm tired, I can just imagine how exhausted she must be. She's old enough to be my mother, she has cancer, and her only daughter was just murdered. Good grief!

She sat down in a chair and took the pad of paper and pen out of her tote. For several moments she sat quietly, making notes of the conversation she'd just had with Marcy Logan. Satisfied she'd captured the essence of the three people Mrs. Logan suspected, she took her phone out of her tote and pressed in Mike's number. She looked at her watch and realized with the time difference, it was noon in Oregon.

Good, she thought. Maybe he can take a break and talk to me for a few minutes.

A moment later she heard the deep voice she'd come to love over the past few years. For a quick moment she reminisced about how she never expected to find romance at this stage of her life. *I'm one of the lucky ones to have a second chance.* She looked up at the ceiling and mentally gave thanks to whatever power was looking out for her.

"Hey, sweetheart, how's Boston treating you?" Mike asked.

"Well, it's a beautiful city, just as you said, and I even took the bus tour. I'm so glad you recommended it, although you weren't the only one. The porter who brought my luggage up to my room also recommended it. Since you answered your phone, I'm assuming you made it back to your office, and you're in the middle of handling all the things that happened during your absence. Would I be right?"

"You certainly would, and you caught me just as I'm beginning to eat a magnificent looking egg salad sandwich I got from the deli up the street."

"I'll let that slide for now. I would have preferred it if you'd gotten something from Kelly's Koffee Shop, but that would be a bit out of the way for you," she said laughing. "Anyway, I'm sure the county is glad to have you back on the job."

"That they are. Now, tell me about Mrs. Logan."

"Mike, she's just about the loveliest person I've ever met. My heart goes out to her for what she must be going through, but even with everything she's dealing with, she was very calm and composed. As a matter of fact, she thinks there are three possible suspects I should look into."

"What the devil do you mean, that you should look into?" Mike asked. Although she couldn't see him she knew he was raising an eyebrow as he spoke.

"Yes, well, I guess I kind of agreed to help her, but I wanted to check with you before I leave for Maine."

"Whoa, Kelly, back up. Start at the beginning. I have no idea why you're even thinking about going to Maine. As I recall, you were going to Boston to talk to Mrs. Logan and then come home. Did I miss something?"

"Not exactly. Here's what she told me." She spent the next twenty minutes telling him about her conversation with Marcy Logan and the three people she thought might have motives for murdering her daughter.

"Kelly, I don't know how this happened," he said in a frustrated tone of voice. "We were supposed to go to Virginia to attend a friend's graduation, and now you're off to Maine to investigate a murder. I guess there's a nexus somewhere, but at the moment I would prefer to have my wife home safe and sound. Rebel, Lady, and Skyy fully agree with me."

"I really miss them, but does that mean you don't want me to go to Maine?" she asked.

"No, I don't want you to go to Maine. Do I think you should? Yes. Mrs. Logan sounds like a good person, and I guess you should do what you can for her. I can't imagine what it must be like to be in her position. I feel for her. I don't know if you'll be able to find out who murdered her daughter, but I think you should try."

"Thanks, Mike. That's pretty much how I feel about it."

"I would suggest, and you realize I'm using the word suggest because I know how much you hate for me to tell you exactly what you should do, but I would suggest you rent a car and take off for Maine in the morning. After you hear from Celia you might want to call the bed and breakfast and reserve a cottage and make a reservation for dinner tomorrow night."

"I have to tell you I'm not real thrilled about driving around on the streets of Boston," Kelly said.

"You can rent a car at the airport and from what I remember, it's pretty close to where you're staying, and then you just head north. It shouldn't be too difficult of a drive. I'm visualizing a map in my head, and I think you're only about an hour or so from where you want to go in Maine."

"Okay, I can do that. I guess the silver lining in all this is I've always wanted to have a lobster dinner in Maine, and now I can."

"Don't forget about the lobster rolls," Mike said. "Remember what that waiter at Bubba's told us. As I recall he said that following the she crab soup and crab cakes at Bubba's the next best thing in the world was a lobster roll."

"I'm sold. The trip will be worth it for the lobster dinner and the lobster roll. I think I should be able to fly back to Portland the day after tomorrow. I'm wondering how I can get back home from Portland. Any chance you can pick me up?"

"Sorry, sweetheart. I'm up to my ears in work. Doc stopped in to say hi this morning and see how the weekend went. He mentioned something about Liz taking this week off. I'll give her a call and see if she can pick you up."

"That would be great. Since she's a psychologist, I'd like to run what Mrs. Logan told me about Clint and Megan by her. While I'm in Portland I also want to stop by Julie's home and see if I can find anything that might shed some light on who the killer might be if it isn't that transient guy. Mike, can I call you back? It looks like I have another call."

"Sure. Talk to you later."

Kelly didn't recognize the number on her phone monitor. "This is Kelly Reynolds."

"Mrs. Reynolds, this is Clint Logan, Marcy Logan's son. I'd like to talk to you. Is there any chance I could meet you at your hotel for dinner this evening? I'm at my mother's home right now, and she told me about your meeting with her."

"Yes, that would be fine. Shall we meet in the lobby at six?"

"I'll be there, and you'll know me by the signature red hair of the Logan family. Julie and I both inherited it from our father. Thanks for seeing me on such short notice."

Kelly called Mike back. "You won't believe this. Guess who I'm meeting for dinner tonight?"

"Knowing you, it's probably someone terribly interesting and terribly important."

"Well, I don't know about how important he is, but it should be interesting."

"Okay," Mike said. "I'll bite. Who is it?"

"I'm meeting Clint Logan, Julie's brother, for dinner here at the hotel restaurant."

"Wow! How did that happen?"

"He was the one on the phone who called a few minutes ago. He said he was at his mother's home, and he wanted to talk to me, so yes, it should be interesting."

"One thing, Kelly. Promise me you won't ask him up to your room. Remember, he's a suspect, and he has a possible motive. I'd feel more comfortable if you'd reassure me you'll stay in a public place all the time with lots of people around."

"Okay, I can promise that. I'll call you when I get back from dinner and tell you all about it. I know you're busy with work-related matters, but I'm sure I'll probably feel like talking to you after I meet Clint. Is that okay?"

"Absolutely. I'll feel much better about you having dinner with him after you call. By the way, I was able to talk to Roxie, and she said not to worry about Kelly's, she'll handle it this week. I also called

Liz, and she'll pick you up at the airport, but you need to text her with your arrival time. She also said she could spend a couple of hours with you at Julie's if you'd like."

"That's a load off my mind. All right. I need to make a few calls, get ready for dinner, and then think about going to Maine tomorrow. I love you, and I'll call you as soon as I get back from dinner."

CHAPTER THIRTEEN

"Hello. This is the law office of Sean O'Brien; how may I help you?" the perky voice that answered the phone said.

"I'd like to speak to Mr. O'Brien. My name is Kelly Reynolds, and this is regarding a client of his, Julie Jensen."

"Are you an attorney, Ms. Reynolds?"

"No, I'm a friend of the family, and I'm afraid I have some bad news regarding Mrs. Jensen."

"Just one moment."

Shortly a male voice with a strong Irish accent came on the line and said, "This is Sean O'Brien, Ms. Reynolds, how may I help you?"

"Mr. O'Brien, I'm sorry to be the bearer of bad news, but your client, Julie Jensen, was murdered in Virginia two days ago. I'm sort of a friend of the family and was at her graduation ceremony in Virginia. She was murdered in her hotel room several hours after the end of the ceremony."

He was quiet for several moments and then he said, "I only met her once when she filled out the necessary divorce papers. I am so sorry. This is terrible news. Have they arrested the murderer?"

Kelly sighed. "The police chief thinks a transient, who had both Julie's jewelry and her wallet in his possession, did it. He wasn't arrested because he was dead when they found him in the hotel parking lot, evidently from an accidental fall. The local police chief is not going to pursue the investigation any further since he believes it's an open and shut case."

"Does the police chief know who Julie's family is? I mean Mrs. Logan is not only one of the wealthiest citizens in Boston, the family is pure blue blood and has been for over two hundred years."

"To be honest, Mr. O'Brien, I don't think he cares. Mrs. Logan does not believe the transient is the one responsible for her daughter's murder, and she's asked me to help."

"Are you a private investigator?"

"No. My husband is the sheriff in Beaver County, Oregon. I've helped him in the past with several murder cases, and a friend of Julie's recommended me to Mrs. Logan. I never had the pleasure of meeting Julie, although, as I said earlier, I did see her receive her doctorate diploma on Saturday. Actually the reason I called is to find out who her attorney is in Portland, Oregon. Mrs. Logan didn't know. I need to notify him, and I'd also like to find out if Julie had a will."

"Certainly. A friend of mine from law school referred her to my office. His name is Ryan Murphy. Here's his telephone number."

"Thank you. No wonder you were friends, being true Irishmen," Kelly said laughing.

"Well, when you're Irish and you want to be a lawyer, it's not too much of a stretch to think of Notre Dame. That's where we met and we received our law degrees. I came back to Boston to practice law, and he returned to his home in Portland, but we've stayed in touch over the years. When you talk to him, please give him my best. I'll wrap up this case. Actually, since there won't be a divorce because one spouse is now deceased, the only thing left to do is get it dismissed."

"Thanks for taking the time to talk to me, and I'll be sure to say hello to Ryan for you."

Kelly looked at the clock on the nightstand and mentally subtracted three hours. It was early afternoon in Portland and hopefully Ryan Murphy would be in his office. She placed the call and a cheerful sounding receptionist said he'd take the call. A few moments later she heard a voice say, "This is Ryan Murphy, Mrs. Reynolds. How can I help you?"

"Mr. Murphy, I'm afraid I have some bad news for you about your client, Julie Jensen. I'm a friend of the Logans, Julie Jensen's family, and I regret to have to tell you that Julie was murdered Saturday evening. I'm in Boston at the moment. A local attorney here by the name of Sean O'Brien gave me your number. By the way, he asked me to say hello to you for him."

He was quiet for a few moments and then he said, "Mrs. Reynolds, I don't know what to say. This is terrible news and comes as a complete shock to me. Julie didn't keep an appointment she'd made for this morning, which was quite unlike her. Now I understand why. Please tell me everything you can."

Kelly recounted the events of the last couple of days and concluded by telling him she planned to return to her home in Oregon sometime in the next few days. "I'd like to ask you a couple of things if you don't mind."

"Certainly, if it's not privileged attorney-client information, I'll answer whatever I can."

"Did you know that Julie's mother gave her a gift of ten million dollars last week?"

There was a sharp intake of breath on the other end of the line. "No, Julie never mentioned that when she made the appointment. Usually my secretary schedules all of my appointments, but she had a parent-teacher conference and had to leave early that day. I was the one who spoke to Julie and scheduled the appointment."

"I know this is a fine line with the attorney-client privilege, but since she's dead and if she has a will, you'll have to file it, and it will then be a public court record. Would I be correct?"

"Yes, she has a will and when we first met she requested that I keep it in a safe place. She said she'd make a new one later on. That's why she made the appointment to see me this morning."

"Do you remember what was in her will? Here's why I'm asking. Her mother is afraid Julie hadn't changed her will and her husband, whom she was divorcing, is still in her will as the prime beneficiary."

"As I recall, that was the case, but I'm not one hundred percent sure. Her will is in a safe deposit box at my bank. When she came to see me about the divorce, I counseled her to draw up a new will. She was uncertain who she should leave her estate to and said she really didn't have all that much, but ten million dollars makes a huge difference, a whole new ball game, if you will."

"I'm going to muddy the waters even more. Did you know Julie had a daughter she put up for adoption at birth with whom she was recently reunited?"

Again there was silence on the other end of the phone. "No, I knew nothing about a daughter. I wonder if she was going to leave her estate to her daughter. Maybe that was the reason for the appointment."

"I have no idea."

"Do you know how to contact her daughter, Mrs. Reynolds, or anything about her?"

"No. I thought when I returned to Oregon I'd spend a little time in Portland and see if there was some way I could gain access to Julie's house. She must have some information regarding her daughter there. The daughter's name is Megan Simmons, she has red hair like Julie did, and she's an attorney specializing in adoption law."

"I think taking a look around her house is a good idea. I have a key to her home. Julie was a very organized person. She told me when she hired me that she'd interviewed several attorneys, and I was the one she'd ultimately chosen, because she trusted me. She told me she wanted to give me a second set of keys to her car, her house, her safe deposit box, everything, because she didn't have any family in Oregon. As far as her daughter being an adoption lawyer, let me see if I can find out anything. I have several friends who specialize in adoption law. Maybe they can tell me something. When are you returning to Oregon?"

"Hopefully, I'm planning on flying into Portland on Wednesday afternoon, but I won't know for sure until tomorrow night or Wednesday morning."

"That's fine. If I'm not here, ask for Sabrina. She's my secretary, and I'll make sure she knows that you can have the key to Julie's house. Is there anything else? Sabrina just handed me a note that my next appointment is out in the reception room and is getting antsy."

"No. I'll let you know what I find out, because whatever I find out will probably have some legal ramifications, particularly since ten million dollars is involved."

"Thank you for calling and yes, please let me know everything you find out. I have a feeling this could get very messy."

"So do I, and again, thanks for taking my call."

CHAPTER FOURTEEN

Promptly at six that evening, Kelly got off the elevator and walked into the lobby. Standing next to the concierge's desk was a man she was sure was Clint Logan. He wore a grey sports coat, a white open necked shirt, and dark blue pants. There are some people in the world who look as if they were born to money, and Clint definitely had that look about him. The two things that kept him from being patrician perfect was the red shock of hair he wore tied in a ponytail and his red goatee. She walked over to him.

"Judging from the color of your goatee and your hair, you must be Clint Logan," she said smiling as she extended her hand.

"That I am, and you must be Mrs. Reynolds," he said shaking her hand. "I made a reservation for us here at the hotel restaurant. I didn't think it would be crowded on a Monday night, which is usually an off night for restaurants, but I understand there's a convention in town tomorrow, so I decided to be safe."

They walked down the hall to the restaurant and as they entered it, the hostess said, "Good evening, Mr. Logan. I have your favorite table ready. It's good to see you. We've missed you." She turned to Kelly and smiled. "That's a beautiful pendant you're wearing."

"Thank you. My husband gave me this emerald drop, because he thought the emerald matched my eyes. I love the way he had it set in a gold bar so it would be heavy enough it wouldn't swing back and forth."

They followed the hostess to their table, and Clint held out Kelly's chair for her. The hostess handed each of them a menu as well as a napkin. "Thanks for saving this table for me, Lisa. I appreciate it," he said to the hostess.

"Well, since you obviously eat here often, what do you recommend besides the Boston cream pie and the Parker House rolls? I overindulged in both of those last night," Kelly said.

"I can't pass up the clam chowder and the scallops. They're two of my favorites. The New England area is known for its seafood, so who am I to argue with that? Plus, today's my birthday, so I'm allowed to indulge," Clint said putting aside his menu.

"Well, happy birthday, and I'll follow your lead. They both sound delicious. Before we go any farther, I want to express my condolences to you on the loss of your sister. It's never easy having a family member die, and particularly under these circumstances."

As she spoke to him, she closely watched to see what his response might be, knowing he was one of the three people who might have had a motive to kill Julie. He ran his hand over his face and said, "No, it's not easy, and it's particularly difficult when you're old and you have cancer. I'm very concerned about my mother. The last thing she needed in her battle with cancer was to have something like this happen."

"Yes, I agree. As you know, I was with her this afternoon, and it's no secret it's taking its toll on her."

They paused while the waiter took their orders. Kelly was surprised when Clint ordered a Perrier with a twist of lime. He seemed more like a fine French wine person. She ordered a chardonnay, and they both ordered the clam chowder and scallops.

"Mother said you were looking into Julie's murder. She's

convinced that someone other than the transient the police found in Virginia is responsible for Julie's death. What do you think?"

Kelly wasn't sure how to answer. She had no idea if Marcy had told Clint about the ten million dollars and her concern that Mark might be a beneficiary under the terms of Julie's will.

"Kelly, it's written all over your face. I sure hope you don't play poker, because a poker face you don't have. You're wondering how much I know. Let me tell you a few things, then I'd like to help you find the murderer.

"I was at Mother's this afternoon after you were there, and I know she told you about my past including my failed marriages and the blow-up my father and I had over his insurance business shortly before his death. She also mentioned she'd told you how she is supporting me. All of that is true. What I don't think she told you, because she's a very proud woman and women of her generation don't usually let their dirty laundry hang out for all to see, is that I'm a recovering alcoholic. I've been sober for several months, and my life has changed dramatically."

"No, your mother didn't mention that to me."

"That doesn't surprise me. My alcoholism was always something she liked to sweep under the rug. Eventually it got to the point where it was affecting every aspect of my life. A month ago, unbeknownst to her, I went to the family insurance company and asked for a job. Mother still owns it even though she has people running it for her. I was hired as a salesman, exactly what my father wanted me to do all those years ago. I'm actually pretty good at it. This afternoon I told mother what I'd done and the fact that I'm seeing a therapist who specializes in the treatment of alcoholism."

"How did she feel about it?"

"She was very supportive, and I think very relieved, that I was finally starting to get my life in order. I even told her I was seeing a woman who wasn't all that attractive," he said laughing. "Beautiful women have not been very good for me, and I say that after three divorces. I recently read something that said the most beautiful mushrooms are also the deadliest. I wouldn't say my wives were deadly, but let's just say they weren't healthy for me."

"That's a good saying. I'll have to remember it."

There's something else, Kelly, and in your eyes this might put me in a position to be a suspect. The counselor I'm seeing believes very much in the twelve step program of Alcoholics Anonymous. One of the steps is making amends. I finally was honest with myself and admitted that probably the major reason Julie and I weren't close was because I was so jealous of her." He paused for a moment and took a sip of his Perrier.

He continued, "You see, I flew down to Virginia early Saturday morning because I wanted to see Julie graduate, and I did."

Kelly took a deep breath and audibly exhaled. "You were at the graduation?"

"Yes, I saw Julie graduate as well as her friend, Stephanie, who I believe is also a friend of yours. I was standing near the back of the crowd. It was a very emotional time for me. After the graduation was over I drove around for a long time thinking about how much my alcoholism had cost me in every aspect of my life. I drove to Virginia Beach, parked my car, and sat looking out at the water for a long time.

"Late that afternoon I drove back to the hotel where I was staying. It's across the street from the university. I decided it was time to apologize to Julie for my past behavior and see if we could start anew. Mother had mentioned she'd be staying at the hotel located on the university grounds. I'm not very proud of this, but patrician looks and a little money can help get a guest's room number from the person at the registration desk.

"I walked over to the building where Julie's room was located, opened the outside door, and stepped into a very long hallway that ran the entire length of the building. Just as I stepped into the hallway, I saw a flash of a person with red hair hurrying away from Julie's room. I was startled because not many people have red hair like mine, and I'm always surprised when I see someone that shares that characteristic."

"You saw someone in the general area of Julie's room with red hair? That is unusual."

"Yes," Clint said struggling to keep his voice even. "I walked to Julie's room, saw the open door, and looked inside. I saw Julie lying in a pool of blood. I assumed she'd been murdered and with my background, I was afraid I'd be a suspect, so I left. I'm not very proud of what I did, but I didn't feel I had a choice. If I'd called the police, I knew they'd detain me. I rushed back to my hotel, drove to the airport, and took the first flight I could get back to Boston." Seemingly emotionally drained, Clint sat back in his chair and took another sip of his Perrier water. Kelly noticed his hand was shaking as he raised the glass to his lips.

He looked at Kelly over his glass and said, "Pretty pathetic, huh?"

"I don't know what to say." Just then the waiter brought their soup and they stopped talking while they enjoyed it. Finally, Kelly spoke. "This is delicious. It really is the best clam chowder I've ever had."

"Wait until you try the scallops. Ahh, perfect timing. Here comes the waiter with our order right now."

After several bites, Kelly said, "Clint, these are every bit as good as the chowder. Thanks for the recommendations."

"Kelly, there's something else you should know," he said putting down his fork. "Mother also told me about the ten million dollars she gave Julie."

Kelly was quiet for a moment and then said, "Forgive me for asking, but did you know anything about it before your mother told you?"

"Of course not. How could I? I haven't seen Julie in a year or so. I didn't want her to see me in the intoxicated condition I was usually in, so I avoided her on her monthly visits to Mother, and she and I haven't talked on the telephone during that time. No, I knew nothing about it."

"How did you feel when you found out?"

He looked at her with eyes that conveyed belief when he said, "The old me would have been furious. The new me understands. I know I'll still inherit a lot from Mother, simply because she has a lot. Actually, I'm fine with it. Julie was a far better daughter than I was a son."

"Did your mother tell you anything else?"

"No, was there more?" he asked, picking up his fork and taking a bite of a scallop.

"Yes. Evidently the daughter Julie gave up for adoption just after she'd graduated from high school found her and they were reunited."

Clint started to stand up and then he sat back down, clearly agitated. "How can that be? I was told the adoption records were sealed."

Kelly explained to him what had happened, then she said, "Your niece has red hair." She waited to see what his reaction would be. He sat slack-jawed for a moment evidently connecting the dots that Kelly had already connected.

"Are you thinking that the red-haired person I saw near Julie's room was her daughter, my niece?" Clint asked as he twisted his napkin tight and laid it on the table.

"Quite honestly, I don't know what to think," she said.

"What do you know about her?" he asked after a few moments had gone by.

"Not much. Her name is Megan Simmons, and she's an attorney specializing in adoption law."

"Do you know where she lives?"

"From what your mother told me, she lives in San Francisco. I plan on going to your sister's home in Portland to see if Julie had any records indicating Megan's address. I'm hoping there will be some information in the house that will be helpful."

"Kelly, I'd like to help. I feel I need to do something, if for no other reason than for my mother. Would you do me a favor?"

"I'll try."

"If I can help in any way, would you please call me? Here's my card with my phone number on it. Feel free to call me at any time. This whole thing is unbelievable. I think I need to go home and process it."

"I'm going to drive to Maine tomorrow to speak with Julie's husband, Mark. It's probably going to be a long day for me, so if you don't mind, I think I'll have to excuse myself. Thank you very much for dinner," Kelly said as she stood up. "I promised my husband I'd call him tonight. I know he was going to bed early since he has a full schedule tomorrow, and I need to get back to my room, so I can make the call. I enjoyed dinner and meeting with you, and I definitely will call you if something comes up. Take care of your mother. She's a very special person."

As she walked to the elevator, a million thoughts tumbled through Kelly's mind. *I wonder if he did know about the ten million dollars, and also isn't seeing a redhead near where his sister was murdered convenient? Maybe the whole thing is too convenient? If he found out Julie's daughter had located her and learned how wealthy her grandmother was it might seriously affect Clint's plans for his future. Megan could possibly lay claim to Julie's estate as well as her grandmother's. If she was successful, it could effectively cut his inheritance even further. I need to find out if Megan was at the graduation. Maybe Mike could call a couple of airlines and see if she was a passenger on a flight to Norfolk, Virginia.* And so her mind started spinning more and more with each new item of information.

*****

Clint watched Kelly as she walked down the hall towards the elevator. When the doors closed behind her he smiled at the waiter and beckoned him over to his table.

"Yes sir, may I get you something?" the waiter asked.

"I'd like a double martini on the rocks."

CHAPTER FIFTEEN

When Kelly walked into her room, she immediately saw the blinking red light on the telephone indicating she had two messages. The first one was from Stephanie asking her to call. The second message was from Julie's attorney in Portland, Ryan Murphy.

She called Stephanie first. "Kelly, what's going on? I've been thinking about you for the last two days. Have you found out anything? What did Mrs. Logan have to say?"

Kelly recounted the events of the last two days to Stephanie ending with a review of her dinner with Clint.

"I know this is going to sound really off the wall, and I know you don't believe in this stuff as much as I do, but is there any way you could get the birth dates for Megan, Clint, and Mark? It might shed some light on the murder."

"Are you kidding, Stephanie? Do you really think you can find out who murdered someone by what you find out from an astrology chart? Seriously?"

"Kelly, I'm not saying it will tell us who did it, but it sure might show that someone had a tendency for violence."

"Okay, just for the record, I'm a non-believer, but I can give you

Megan's birth date and Clint's. According to Mrs. Logan, Megan was born on October 20, 1986. Clint was born on May 23rd. Today's his birthday."

"Wow, Kelly, that's great. Do you know the year he was born?"

"I think I can figure it out. He's seven years younger than Julie, and she was forty-six when she died, so he must have been born in 1977. Does that help?"

"Tremendously. Let me do a little research. I'll email you what I find out, since it will probably be a couple of hours before I can get to it. One more thing. When you go to York to see Mark tomorrow, see if you can get his birthdate information."

Kelly let out a big sigh. "I'll try, but I can't promise anything."

"Okay. By the way, I may have another suspect for you."

"What?" Kelly practically screamed through the phone. "Who?"

"I told you how I hired Julie to work for me after I'd met her during the doctoral program and seen how smart she was and the type of work she did."

"Yes, I remember."

"Well, I'd been mentoring a woman, Sophie Marx, for several years and she worked directly under me, actually she's the one who would have probably been chosen as my replacement when I retire if it hadn't of been for Julie. Her credentials were stronger and she became the second in command. Sophie worked for her. I guess you could say she was demoted. She has a master's degree, and made a lot of snide comments to people about Julie getting her doctorate.

"One of the secretaries told me today that Sophie mentioned to her that it was a good thing Julie wasn't around anymore because now things could get back to normal. The secretary also told me that last week Sophie had commented to her that Julie should have a bad accident. Sounded kind of ominous to me."

"Well, I can understand someone being concerned about their job in that instance, but I hardly see where that qualifies her to be a candidate for being a murder suspect."

"Kelly, here's the thing. I looked at her astrology chart today and it showed a transiting Mars and a transiting Pluto conjunct in natal Sun/Saturn opposition in the 8th house at the same time that an eclipse was happening in the 8th house. That's really malefic."

"Stephanie, I don't have a clue about what you just said, and I have no idea what malefic means. You know I don't have a doctorate. Matter of fact, as you may remember, high school was as good as it got for me."

"You don't need a doctorate, Kelly. What it means is that when those two planets are in that alignment it can cause an unfavorable influence."

"Again, I find it hard to believe that the date when someone was born could contribute to their tendency to be a murderer."

"You might not think that, Kelly, but a lot of people do, and take it from me, it bears looking into. I checked with Human Resources, and Sophie was out last Friday, supposedly sick."

"So you think there's a chance she flew to Virginia on Friday and murdered Julie? Is that what you're saying?" Kelly asked incredulously. "I suppose the stars are also telling you she was wearing a red wig."

"Because we're friends, I'm going to ignore that snide comment. I'm not accusing anyone of anything, but you have to agree, that's quite a coincidence," Stephanie said.

"I would agree it's quite a coincidence. I'm going to call Mike in a couple of minutes after I make another call. It seems to me he has a contact at the Portland airport, and maybe he can find out if a particular person took a flight out of Portland on a certain date. I'll ask him about Sophie."

"If she did fly there, it still doesn't mean she murdered Julie, but if she didn't fly there, we can eliminate her," Stephanie said.

"I agree. I'll look forward to your email and thanks. Although I don't understand your astrology, that doesn't mean it isn't worth taking a look at. I'll talk to you in a day or so," Kelly said.

"Drive safely tomorrow. I've never met Mark, but even though he and Julie were going through a divorce, I never heard her say anything bad about him, which is pretty unusual."

"I'm looking forward to meeting him, and I'm looking forward to Maine. I've never been there before."

"From what I hear," Stephanie said, "the lobster rolls at the hole in the wall eateries is the way to go. Have one for me."

"Will do!"

*****

Kelly pressed in the number that Ryan Murphy had left in his message and a moment later she heard him say, "Thanks for calling me back, Mrs. Reynolds. I found out something I think you'll find interesting."

"I'm a bit overwhelmed at this point because there's so much about Julie's murder that's interesting, but please, tell me what you've found out."

"I called several of my friends who are adoption law attorneys. Two of them were no help, but the third one had just returned from a court appearance in a bitter adoption case. Evidently an Indian tribe in south Oregon was claiming that a six-year old child who was a member of the tribe and had been adopted by Anglo parents should be returned to the tribe so she could be raised by them. The adoptive parents would have to give her up. He's representing the adoptive parents. His opposing counsel was a red-haired woman by the name of Megan Simmons. He told me even though she's only thirty, she's already a legend in legal circles."

"Well, five will get you ten that's Julie's daughter. The age is right and the red hair definitely makes it sound like it's her. Did you find out where she lives or works?"

"She lives in San Francisco, but she's licensed to practice law in several western states, and because of her reputation, she's very much in demand. I called her law office and found out she will be in Portland the rest of this week and next week, representing clients, and meeting with potential clients. At least that's what her secretary said."

"I know this is a long shot, but did you find out where she's staying while she's in Portland?"

"Yes. She's at the Heathman Hotel in downtown Portland."

"Thank you so much, Ryan. I still want to go to Julie's house, but you certainly confirmed what Julie's mother said about Megan living in San Francisco. I really appreciate your call."

"Happy to help. Julie was my client, so I feel I have an obligation to do what I can in this case. Don't forget to call me, so I can give you the key to Julie's house."

"I won't. I'm leaving for Maine in the morning, but if it goes as planned, I should be returning to Portland Wednesday afternoon. Again, thanks."

CHAPTER SIXTEEN

Kelly looked at the clock on the nightstand, and although it was nine at night on the East Coast, it was only six o'clock in Cedar Bay. She planned on getting an early start in the morning, but she'd promised Mike she'd give him a call after her dinner with Clint. Hoping he was at home, she pressed his number into her cell phone.

"Kelly, I was just thinking about you while I was feeding the dogs. I think they all miss you, although Skyy does seem to be a dog that's loyal to whoever is feeding her at the moment."

"I'm not surprised. Think she's still a little too young to have developed a strong sense of loyalty to either one of us. I'm hoping that will come. I'm always afraid if someone offers her a treat, she'd be gone in a minute. I'm even hesitant to take her with me and leave her in the car when I run errands. The vet told me to be careful because with her show dog looks, he was afraid someone might try to steal her. If they had a dog treat, she'd probably go willingly."

"Enough about the dogs, love. I miss you. Are you still planning on coming home Wednesday?"

"I am, barring anything unforeseen happening. If you have a minute, I'd like to bring you up to date on everything that's going on with this case."

"Sweetheart, now that the dogs have been fed, I can listen to you uninterrupted. Otherwise, I might have had a riot on my hands. It was a brutal day at work, so if you hear strange gurgling sounds, it's just me pouring myself a glass of wine. I want to hear about everything, and since you're calling I assume your dinner worked out."

"Well, yes, but I have some doubts. Okay here goes." She spent the next twenty minutes telling him about her dinner with Clint and the conversations she'd had with Stephanie and Ryan. "What do you think, Mike? You know how much I value your input."

"Thanks for the compliment, but sweet talk isn't going to take away the feeling I'm getting that you're putting yourself in danger. I have some real reservations about this guy Clint. Everything is a little too smooth. I mean the guy's life has been a mess in every respect, and suddenly he has a flash from above or somewhere, and he decides to completely change? Then his sister is mysteriously murdered, and that happens just a few days after she's been given ten million dollars.

"Need I remind you if Mrs. Logan hadn't given that amount to Julie, it would probably have been split between Julie and him at the time of her death. And he just happens to see someone with red hair not too far from where Julie was murdered? And he says he knew nothing about having a red-haired niece? Kelly, his whole story seems too coincidental and too pat for me. What was your impression of him? Not based on what he told you, your gut reaction."

She was quiet for a few moments as she thought about it. "Mike, I can't really answer your question one way or the other. I have a feeling something is off, but I don't know what it could be. Certainly he said all the right things, and if he is trying to get his life together, I applaud him for that, but on the other hand, I have to agree with you. His story does seem pretty convenient. I'm not sure how to go about finding out whether or not it's true. I certainly can't just show up at the insurance company and ask if he's working there or peek in a window to see if he really isn't drinking."

"You're resourceful. You'll think of something. Kelly, I don't mean to cut you off, but I've got some work I need to do on the computer. Are you set for Maine tomorrow?"

"Yes, I've reserved a car and made a reservation at the Harbor House Bed and Breakfast. That's the one Julie's husband owns. I looked it up on the Internet, and I reserved a cottage. It looks charming, and it's right on the water. Anyway, I plan on eating breakfast here at the hotel and then I'll drive up there.

"When I made my reservation, the clerk told me if I took I-95 it would take me close to an hour and a half, but she suggested I take Route 1A to Beverly and then take Route 127 north. It will take me longer, but she said it was really a scenic drive along the coast, and I could also see the marshes and some of the other cities I've read about. Matter of fact, I read a book by Nelson DeMille years ago called Plum Island, and the actual island is on the route I'll be taking. As long as I'm going there, I might as well see everything I can."

"I couldn't agree more. I read that book, too, and as I remember it was pretty good. I'll be curious what you think about that part of the country. Anything else before I sign off?"

"Yes, one more thing. I seem to recall you have a contact at the Portland Airport. I'd like to know if Megan or Sophie flew to Norfolk, Virginia last Friday? Any chance you can find that out for me?" Kelly asked.

"I do have a contact there who has been very helpful in the past. Since the murdered woman lived in Portland, I can probably get him to search the airline manifests of the different airlines and see what he can come up with. Give me the names."

"Sophie Marx and Megan Simmons, and please thank him for me."

"Nope, don't think he'd do it for someone else, even as charming and beautiful as you are. I'll couch it in such a way he'll think he's doing me a huge favor and one he can collect back from me when it's needed. What I've done in the past is send him a case of wine. He's quite the connoisseur."

"That shouldn't be a problem. I'll take care of it when I get back. Mrs. Logan offered to pay me to find out who killed her daughter, and although I wouldn't take money for doing it, I'm not averse to being reimbursed for costs."

"Give me a call sometime tomorrow or tomorrow night. I know you're planning on talking to Julie's ex-husband, and I'll be curious to hear what you think of him. Do you have a plan?"

"No, I'll just have to play it by ear. I hope this trip isn't in vain."

"Kelly, don't forget to find out his birthday," he said sarcastically. "I'm sure that's terribly important, at least Stephanie thinks so."

"You can lose the attitude, Mike. Stephanie and a lot of other people really believe in astrology, and who am I to say there's nothing to it?"

"Right, Kelly, right. Keep on believing that, but let me give you a little free advice. Don't tell this guy Mark that you want to know his date of birth, just so you can tell someone who believes in astrology. Don't think you'd come off sounding very professional if you did that."

"You're probably right. Love you and talk to you tomorrow. I'm going to bed."

"And I'm off to defrost and heat one of those casseroles you always have on hand in the freezer. I saw one in there that's calling my name."

"Which one is that?"

"The one labeled chicken and spinach crepes with a mushroom sauce.

"Enjoy. Sleep well."

CHAPTER SEVENTEEN

The next morning Kelly packed the last of her clothes in her suitcase, walked out of her room, and down the hall to the elevator. A few moments later she walked into the restaurant.

"I see you're wearing that beautiful pendant I commented on last night," the hostess said. "Will Mr. Logan be joining you for breakfast or are you dining alone?" she asked.

"Thank you for noticing, and I'll be eating by myself." The hostess walked across the room and seated Kelly at a small booth.

"You seem to know Mr. Logan quite well. I just met him last night. What can you tell me about him?" Kelly asked, hoping she was being resourceful, as Mike liked to think she was.

"I don't know much about him. He's been coming here for several years, at least as long as I've been a hostess here. He usually has a different woman with him each time. I don't know if he's married or not, but he's a very good tipper."

"Yes, I've heard that people who are heavy drinkers are usually good tippers, but now that he's not drinking, has that affected the amount he tips?"

"That may be true for some people, but since he's still drinking he still tips well."

"Really, I thought he'd quit drinking," Kelly said.

"Not that I know of. He was here quite late last night drinking double martinis. Actually Billy, the bartender, told me he had to quit serving him, because he was getting sloppy drunk. He arranged with the doorman to get a taxi for him. It's a good thing he never drives when he comes here, because I wouldn't want to be on the street after he leaves. Excuse me, some people just walked in. I need to seat them."

"Thanks, Lisa."

Well, that's interesting. He certainly lied to me about that. I wonder if everything else he told me was a lie.

*****

Although Kelly had been dreading renting the car and driving in Boston, she was surprised at how smoothly it had gone. Within fifteen minutes she was on the outskirts of Boston and on her way to Maine. After the reservation clerk told her about the scenic coastal drive, she never even considered taking the Interstate all the way to York. Marshes, the ocean, Plum Island, and charming little cities, one after another, comprised her drive.

When she got to Kittery, Maine, she stopped at a drugstore to get some contact lens eye drops. She'd had enough to last her over the weekend, but with the added days of the trip, she knew she was close to running out. "Passing thru or gonna stay awhile? See ya' got a rental car," the grizzled clerk said.

"I'm on my way to York, and yes, I'm just passing through. I've been told that this is the area where I can get great lobster rolls. I own a coffee shop in Oregon, so I'm always on the lookout for good food."

"Ya' won't find none better than at Josie's place next door. I've been gettin' one every day longer than I care to count. She serves 'em up with her homemade potato salad. She's won some contests, and she's been written up in 'bout every paper around. Once she even made the Boston Globe. Service is a mite slow, but trust me, it's worth the wait."

"Thanks, fortunately I'm not in a hurry. I think I'll take your suggestion and go next door and try one."

"Ya' won't regret it. Tell her Sol sent ya'. Need a bag for them eye drops?"

"No, I'll just put them in my purse, and I'll be sure and tell her you sent me. Thanks again."

Kelly put the eye drops in her purse and went next door to the tiny nondescript diner. There were six wooden tables with chairs sitting on an old linoleum floor, that from the discoloration and stains, looked like it had been the original flooring. The wooden counter was marked with cigarette burns and it too, looked like the original one. Each table had a Mason jar on it containing brightly colored flowers.

"Are you Josie?" she asked the middle-aged woman standing behind the counter dressed in worn jeans and a dark blue t-shirt with the word "Kittery" emblazoned on it in white letters. Her brown hair with flecks of grey was pulled back in a high ponytail.

"That I am. And you are?"

"My name's Kelly. Sol next door said you make the best lobster rolls around. I've never had one, and I'm really looking forward to eating one."

"Well, Kelly, you've come to the right place. Been makin' them since I was old enough to stand behind this counter with my mother who ran this joint before I took over. People tell me they're purty good," she said modestly. "Have a seat, and I'll bring you one."

"How much do I owe you?"

"I'll collect it after ya' eat it. Ain't never had no one not pay because they didn't like it, but I'm sure there'll come a time, and if they don't like it, don't want 'em payin' me anyway."

Kelly walked over to a table and sat down thinking, *that would never happen in a big city. I'm definitely in another part of the world.*

Ten minutes later Josie put a huge split hot dog bun filled with chunky lobster and a side of potato salad in front of Kelly. "Wow, this looks delicious. Thank you!"

"Just a pile of fresh lobster, mayo, celery, lemon juice, and some chives. Easy peasy. See ya' helped yerself to some water outta the case. Can I get ya' anything else?"

"Just a little time. I'm going to enjoy every bite of this," Kelly said as Josie walked back to the counter to take the orders of a man and woman who had walked in.

Halfway through the roll, Kelly made her mind up to try and reinvent the recipe at her coffee shop in Oregon. *I know the freshness of the lobster has something to do with it, and mine might never compare to this, but I'd bet not too many people who come to my coffee shop have had the real deal. It's definitely worth a try.*

When she was finished she walked over to the counter. Josie slid a handwritten piece of paper with the amount Kelly owed across the counter. "Well, honey, what did you think of it?" she asked.

"It was fantastic. I'm going to try and duplicate it when I get home, but I know I'll never be able to make one quite like this. Thank you so much. I'm so glad I didn't go to some fancy schmancy restaurant and pay an arm and a leg and then be disappointed. This is definitely a highlight of my trip."

"Glad you enjoyed it. Ever get back to these parts, don't be a stranger, hear?"

"Thanks, and I promise if I'm ever this way again, your lobster roll will be a priority!"

CHAPTER EIGHTEEN

When Kelly got to the city limit sign for York, Maine, she plugged in the address of the Harbor House Bed and Breakfast on the car's GPS and followed the directions from the anonymous voice. Within minutes she entered a lane that led to a large white clapboard house with a wraparound porch and five detached cottages, all of which looked out at the protected harbor. In front of the main house was a white sign that said "Welcome to Harbor House Bed and Breakfast" in green letters.

She parked her car under a large tree, and as soon as she stepped out of the car she could smell the saltwater, which wasn't all that different from what she smelled when she stepped outside her home on the bluff overlooking Cedar Bay, Oregon. It was a clear sunny day, and she paused for a moment watching the boats bobbing in the harbor.

Next to the screen door was a sign that said "Registration." She entered the house and walked over to a dutch door that had the word "Registration" above it. A large antique grandfather clock flanked the lower half of the dutch door which had been converted into a small counter. A buzzer and a note on it asked guests to press it for service. A moment later a young woman walked out from a room behind the counter and asked, "May I help you?"

"Yes, my name is Kelly Reynolds, and I have a reservation for tonight."

"Of course. You were the one who was driving up from Boston. How was your drive?"

"I thoroughly enjoyed it. Thanks for the recommendation to take the scenic route, but I think the best part of it was the lobster roll I had in Kittery at a place called Josie's."

"If you ate at Josie's you definitely had the best lobster roll in these parts. She and her restaurant are an institution. You couldn't have done better. Here's the key to cottage #5. It's early in the season and so far, only one other cottage has been rented, so if you're looking for a little quiet time, I think you'll definitely find it here, plus, cottage #5 is at the far end."

"That sounds great. I know it's early in the season, but will the restaurant be serving dinner tonight?"

"Yes, although it is early, we have a lot of locals who look forward to our restaurant opening the first of May. We also have a continental breakfast for our guests in the dining room in the morning, beginning at 7:30."

"Thanks. If you take reservations for dinner, I'd like you to put me down for six-thirty tonight. Is that possible?"

"Not only possible, but done."

Kelly looked out at the ocean and said, "The view is just beautiful. You must enjoy working here."

"I do, but I just hope it doesn't close," the young woman said.

"Why would it close?" Kelly asked. "When I read the blurb about it on the Internet it said the Harbor House had been owned by the same family for three generations. I can't imagine they'd think about closing it."

The young woman looked around to see if anyone was within hearing distance and then whispered to Kelly, "They don't want to close it, it's just that the last couple of years have been rough financially. When the economy is down, people don't come to bed and breakfasts in Maine. I understand the owner is very close to bankruptcy."

"I'm sorry to hear that. I seem to recall that his name was Jessup or Jensen, something like that."

"It's Jensen, Mark Jensen."

"Now I remember. Is he here today?"

"No. He left a little while ago. Rather than have the supplies delivered by a commercial delivery truck, he's started going to the suppliers to pick them up and save on the freight charges. He told me he'd probably stay in Boston for dinner and avoid the traffic. He said he'd be back around 8:30 or so tonight."

"In that case, I probably won't have a chance to meet him tonight, but please tell him how charming I think his bed and breakfast is. Thanks again, you've been very helpful."

Kelly walked along the stone path bordered by budding spring plants to cottage #5 and unlocked the door. She entered a small room with a closet and a dresser. Off to the right was the bathroom and directly in front of her was the bedroom which had sliding glass doors that looked out at the water. The sunlight danced on the water, creating what looked like moving golden jewels as the tide rose and fell.

The décor of the cottage was chic maritime. Nautical prints were above the bed which had a quilt with white boats on a blue background with red accents. The color theme was repeated throughout the cottages. Even the shower curtain had a nautical motif.

Given the theme, I'm surprised the windows aren't portholes, Kelly thought as she walked out the door to retrieve her luggage. *I have to give Mark a five star rating on the maintenance and upkeep of the property. Even though it sounds like he's in serious financial trouble, you'd never know it by looking around. Everything is freshly painted, planted, and groomed. It would be a shame to see this beautiful place sold or closed.*

Kelly opened the glass doors and sat down in one of the chairs on the small patio. She got her phone out of her purse and took several pictures, wanting to share the beauty of the view with Mike when she returned to Cedar Bay. She spent the next hour making notes about everything she'd learned regarding Julie, including her conversation with Mrs. Logan and her suspicions about Mark, Clint, and Megan.

Kelly was still uncertain about what to think of Clint. She had a hard time believing that everything he'd told her was a lie, but then there was the conversation with the hostess at the hotel restaurant earlier in the day. The hostess had no reason to lie about Clint's alcohol intake the evening before. When she was finished, she reviewed her notes and couldn't come to any conclusions. In her mind, and in Mrs. Logan's mind, Mark, Clint, and Megan all seemed to have reasons for wanting to see Julie dead. Stephanie thought that Sophie might be another suspect. That made four people who might have murdered Julie, but which one, if any? She had no answer.

She had no way of knowing if any of them or all of them knew about the ten million dollars, although in Sophie's case, that didn't seem to be relevant. If it was Mark, he'd have to know that Julie hadn't changed her will. If it was Clint, he'd have to know that Mrs. Logan had gifted ten million dollars to her daughter. If it was Megan, she'd have to prove she was the rightful heir to the ten million dollars, although that might create a real legal battle between Mark and Megan. Who would be the legal heir in that case? Can a child given up for adoption successfully claim she's an heir when her biological parent dies? She decided to ask Ryan about that when she saw him in Portland. Her mind was going in circles, and she was getting nowhere. She took a book out of her tote bag and read into the late afternoon sun, simply relaxing, a rare thing in the life of Kelly Reynolds.

Reluctantly, she put her book on the nightstand at 6:00 and changed clothes. She wasn't sure if there was a dress code for dinner at a place like this, but jeans might not make it. As she walked towards the main house she noticed that the parking lot was full.

Guess the receptionist wasn't kidding when she told me the locals liked the food here. Think lobster will be my choice tonight. I can't come to Maine and not have a lobster dinner.

She entered the restaurant, walked up to the hostess station, and said, "I have a reservation. My name is Kelly Reynolds. It looks like you're doing a very good business this evening."

"Right this way, Mrs. Reynolds. Yes, although it's very early in the season, the local people eagerly wait for the restaurant to open each year. Here's your table. Daniel, your waiter, will be with you in a moment," she said handing Kelly a menu.

A moment later a young man dressed in black pants with a white shirt approached her table and said, "I'm Daniel. May I get you something to drink while you look over the menu?"

"Yes, I'd like a glass of chardonnay wine. If you have a recommendation, that would be fine."

"A lot of our guests are partial to the Rombauer chardonnay. I think you'd enjoy it's soft, buttery taste," he said.

"Yes, that's a good choice. I've had it before, and it's one of my favorites." When he walked away she thought it was a good thing Mrs. Logan was paying her out-of-pocket costs, given the fact she'd just ordered a glass of a very expensive wine. Also, since the menu indicated the lobster was "market price," it didn't sound like it was going to be cheap, either. Along with the lobster, which was topped with a warm brandy lobster cream sauce, she opted for an appetizer of blue mussels simmered in chardonnay with herbs, garlic, tomatoes, and served with a warm baguette. When Daniel returned with her wine, she gave him her order, thoroughly looking forward to the next hour.

As she swallowed the last bite of the lobster she thought, *no wonder people come to Maine from all over the world just for the lobster. That was one of the most fabulous meals I've ever had. I'm absolutely stuffed. I couldn't eat one more thing.*

"It looks like you enjoyed your lobster. May I recommend dessert?" Daniel asked as he removed her plate from the table.

"You did just fine with the wine recommendation and the dinner was superb. I'm stuffed, but since I probably won't pass this way again, what do you suggest?"

"Just before my shift started, I had the sliced apples baked with cinnamon and sugar. It's covered with a brown sugar and oatmeal mixture and topped with whipped cream. I really think you'd like it."

"If I have to call 911 tonight for overdosing on rich food, may I also call you?" she asked laughing. "Yes, I'll try it, although I'm sure I'll regret it in the middle of the night."

When Kelly walked back to her cottage, she noticed the new moon which was just peeping out, and she was glad she'd left the porchlight on even though it was still twilight. The only other light came from the parking lot and a few small twinkling lights along the stone path that led to her cottage.

She unlocked the door to her cottage and gratefully changed into a non-binding nightgown and robe, filled beyond full with delicious food, but having no regrets.

CHAPTER NINETEEN

After Kelly had changed clothes and gotten relatively comfortable, she checked her cell phone for messages. There was one from Stephanie asking her to call. She punched in the numbers and heard Stephanie's voice say, "I'm glad you called. How's Maine?"

"It's beautiful. I'm in a small cottage overlooking a harbor, and I just had one of the best meals of my life, although I'm stuffed almost to the point of being sick to my stomach. I knew when I ate the meal I'd probably regret it, but I'd do it all over again. What's up in Portland?"

"I wanted to run something by you. Sophie Marx made an appointment to see me this afternoon. I felt really uncomfortable after our meeting."

"Why, you're the boss? How can an employee make you feel uncomfortable?"

"Sophie wanted to know when I was going to name her to replace Julie. She specifically said, 'Julie is dead, and that's probably a good thing, because a lot of people around here think you made a mistake when you brought her on two years ago, and demoted me.' I'm not sure I want to promote anyone who has that kind of an attitude, and I have to say, she still could be a suspect."

"I agree with you. I'd have trouble working with anyone who said something like that, but that doesn't mean she committed murder."

"I know, Kelly, it just seems awfully coincidental. I mean Julie gets her doctorate which is a big deal in this industry, particularly in her specialty. That practically assured her appointment as my successor when I retire. Although Sophie is more qualified than anyone else here, she doesn't have a doctorate. What if she murdered Julie, so she would no longer be a threat to her?"

"I suppose it's possible, but it would have been difficult. The time line for her would be awfully tight. She'd have to fly to the East Coast on Friday, murder Julie on Saturday, fly back to Portland Saturday evening or Sunday, and show up for work on Monday. That's a jam-packed schedule. I'd be surprised if she could have pulled it off.

"I haven't talked to Mike yet regarding the airline manifests, but he thought he could probably find out if her name appeared on any of the manifests maintained by the airlines. Of course, if she didn't use her real name, and had a fake driver's license or passport, we'll never know if she flew to Norfolk."

"Yeah," Stephanie said, sighing. "I'm in a real bind here. On one hand, I probably should appoint Sophie to fill Julie's position, but on the other hand, I don't feel I can work with her if she has that kind of an attitude."

"Well, Steph, you're the one getting paid the big bucks, and I think that's one of the reasons you're getting them. Someone has to make the tough decisions, and it looks like it's you. If Mike finds out anything, I'll let you know, otherwise I think we're at a dead end with her."

"I suppose you're right. What's on your agenda for tomorrow? Coming home?"

"I'm hoping to have a chance to talk to Julie's ex-husband in the morning. He's in Boston this evening and won't return until later tonight. After that I'm planning on returning to Boston and getting the first flight I can to Portland."

"Who's going to pick you up?"

"A friend of ours has this week off, so Mike asked her. I'm also going to meet with Julie's attorney while I'm there. He has the key to her house, and I'm hoping I can find something there that might shed some light on this case. Suspects on both coasts makes it a bit frustrating. Oh, I forgot to tell you something about Clint, Julie's brother." She spent the next few minutes relating her morning conversation with the restaurant hostess and what she said about Clint.

"So what do you make of that, Kelly?"

"I don't know. Maybe he'd given up alcohol, but after our conversation he relapsed. I just don't know. I suppose it's another piece to the puzzle."

"This is one of those jigsaw puzzles where it's not too hard to get the corners and the sides done, but filling in the middle is the real challenge."

"Good analogy, Steph. I'll keep it in mind. I need to call Mike. If he's found out anything about Sophie, I'll text you. I'll talk to you in a day or two."

She ended the call, walked into the bathroom, and took an Alka-Seltzer tin foil pouch out of her travel cosmetic bag. *I don't think I've had one of these in ten years, but I really overdid it tonight. I don't feel guilty, just stuffed beyond the point of satisfaction. One every ten years can't hurt me.* She opened the packet and dissolved it in the recommended four ounces of water and drank it. *Within minutes she felt better. I don't care if it's a placebo or not, it seems to work. Now I need to call Mike.*

When Mike answered the phone, she heard his deep masculine voice say, "Hi, sweetheart, how was the drive up from Boston? Did you get to eat a lobster roll?"

"The drive was beautiful, and although I'm sorry someone had to be murdered for me to do it, I'm glad I had the opportunity. And yes, I ate a lobster roll and it was fantastic. I also just ate the biggest meal of my life, and I had to take an Alka-Seltzer to keep from getting sick."

"Kelly, that is so unlike you. What did you have for dinner?"

She told him what she'd eaten and when she finished, he said, "This is killing me. You know what I'm having tonight?"

"I have no idea, and you're not going to make me feel guilty for sharing my extravagance with you. You're the one who asked."

"You're right, but I want you to know I'll thinking of you when I open my lone can of tuna."

"Mike, as much food as there is in that freezer at home, you have more than enough to eat."

"I know, Kelly, I know, just teasing. So what else happened today?"

"Well, I started off by having an interesting conversation with the hostess in the hotel dining room this morning. Here's what she told me."

When she was finished telling Mike what Lisa, the hostess, had told her she asked, "What do you make of that?"

"Could be two things. He may never have quit drinking, at least that's what the hostess indicated, but I thought you said last night that the hostess mentioned they'd missed him, because he hadn't eaten there lately. If that's true, maybe he just reacted to what you told him by doing what he'd done in the past, drinking himself into oblivion."

"Yes, that possibility crossed my mind, but I wonder if he lied to me, and he never quit drinking?"

"I don't know how you're going to find that out, but if it's true, then everything else he told you could just as well have been a lie."

"That thought kept crossing my mind on my drive up here. Right now, I don't know which one to believe, and I don't know how I'd find out which one is the truth."

"I don't either unless you returned to Boston and talked to people who know him, but I think that's above and beyond what you've agreed to do for Mrs. Logan. I thought of something today. Has anyone told Julie's daughter, Megan, that Julie has been murdered?"

"Not to my knowledge. I think Ryan is the only one who knows her full name and where she lives and works and also knows that her mother is dead. Actually I'd like to talk to her when I get to Portland tomorrow. Ryan gave me the name of her hotel. I thought I'd call and introduce myself as both a friend of her grandmother's and someone who had attended her mother's graduation. What do you think of that?"

"As always, I'm concerned for your safety. You don't have Rebel with you, and you don't have a gun with you. What's the name of that attorney you're going to meet with tomorrow?"

"His name is Ryan Murphy. Why?"

"I just want to call him, and introduce myself. Tell him I'm a sheriff, and see if I can help him with anything."

"Mike, that doesn't sound at all like you. Why are you really going to call him?"

He was quiet for a moment, and then he said, "I'm going to ask him if he can get you a gun. I want you to have some sort of protection."

"Don't you even think about it! Good grief, he'd probably think we were both nut cases. The only thing on my agenda when I land in Portland is to meet Ryan and go to Julie's house. I might ask him to come with me to meet with Megan, but that's it. No, I definitely don't want you to call him. Promise?"

"All right. On another subject, have you had a chance to meet with Julie's ex-husband?"

"No. Here's why." She filled him in on her conversation with the receptionist at the bed and breakfast and how she'd hinted strongly that the property was in financial trouble.

"So you think you can meet with him in the morning?"

"I sure hope so. That's the main reason I'm here. Mike, this property is beautifully maintained. He may be having trouble financially, but you'd never know it. Everything's been freshly painted, flowers have been planted, and no expense was spared in getting top quality ingredients for the meal I was served."

"Kelly, I'm going to have to go. The dogs are circling the campfire. In other words, each one of them is whimpering letting me know it's time for their dinner. Be safe, and I'll see you tomorrow night."

"Mike, one more question. Were you able to find out if Sophie or Megan flew to Norfolk last Friday?"

"Yes, sorry, it slipped my mind with everything else. Sophie Marx did fly to Norfolk, Virginia on Friday. She returned to Portland Saturday night. That's all I know. Megan's name was not on the manifest lists, but she might have used a false ID and made the reservation under that name. I don't know what to make of Sophie, but it certainly makes her a suspect worth looking into. Why don't you have Stephanie make an appointment with her for Thursday afternoon? You could sit in and say you have evidence that she flew to Norfolk, Virginia. Ask her why she flew there and see what she says. No matter what you find out, you're going to have to buy the case of wine for my contact. Matter of fact, I told him it would be coming."

"Oh my gosh! That definitely puts her right near the top of the suspect list. Stephanie had a feeling about Sophie based on her astrology stuff. Maybe there's something to it. Your idea of a meeting with her is a good one. When I get off the phone I'll text Stephanie and tell her to set up the meeting with Sophie. Give the dogs a hug and a kiss for me and tell them I'll be home tomorrow night."

"Hugs and kisses are fine for them, but I'm expecting a little more," he said suggestively.

"You're incorrigible," she said laughing. "Sleep well."

CHAPTER TWENTY

Kelly got in bed and texted Stephanie with what Mike had found out. She asked her to set up a meeting with Sophie for Thursday afternoon which would give Kelly time to drive back to Portland from Cedar Bay. She took the book she'd been reading earlier from the nightstand and started reading, hoping a little quiet time would help her digest her dinner. She read for two hours, then reached up and turned off the lamp above her head. The bed was comfortable, and she rolled over on her side, looking forward to a good night's sleep.

She was almost asleep when she heard something that sounded like a footstep near the small window next to her bed. She froze, wishing she had her dogs with her. They always alerted her when someone was on the property. Every sense in her body was heightened and on edge as she lay perfectly still, painfully aware she was completely defenseless. Listening intently, she heard the sound again. She was sure someone was outside her window.

A moment later a man's voice yelled loudly, "Hey, what are you doing out there? Get off my property." A dog started growling and barking outside and from the sound of it the dog wasn't too far from her cottage and seemed to be getting closer. She heard the sound of someone running away from the window and moments later a car engine roared to life, and then she heard a vehicle speeding down the lane away from the bed and breakfast. She tried to slow her beating heart down, knowing at her age, a heart racing that fast, particularly after a huge meal, was a recipe for disaster. She took several deep breaths, trying to calm herself.

A few moments later there was a knock on the door, and she heard a man's voice say, "Mrs. Reynolds, it's Mark Jensen. I'm the owner of Harbor House. Are you all right? Please open the door."

"Just a moment. Let me get a robe on," Kelly answered. She opened the door and came face to face with Julie's ex-husband who was holding a pistol in his hand. A yellow labrador retriever stood next to him, panting. "What is this all about?" she asked.

"I have no idea. I returned from Boston, did some work in my office and started to go upstairs to bed. I happened to look out the window on the landing as I was going upstairs and thought I saw someone moving in the shadows near your cottage. I watched for a moment, and whoever it was looked like he was wearing a mask to cover his face. The person was dressed entirely in black which I thought was strange. The person crept to the far side of your cottage, went around the corner, and then disappeared. I think it was a man.

"I collared Max and grabbed my gun," he said looking down at the yellow lab who was straining at his leash, clearly wanting to have a chance to chase after whoever he'd seen. "I yelled for the person to get off my property. I saw him running away, and a moment later I heard a car engine start. Are you having any issues with someone? Are you being stalked?"

"No, I know as little about this as you do. Please come in and sit down. I was hoping to talk to you tomorrow. Max is welcome to come in, too. I have a yellow lab at home, and I sure wish she'd been with me tonight, as well as a couple of other dogs my husband and I own."

"You wanted to talk to me? Why?" Mark asked with a quizzical look on his face, as he sat down on one of the chairs that flanked the sliding glass doors overlooking the water. Max laid down next to him, and Mark absentmindedly petted his head.

"Mr. Jensen, a woman by the name of Stephanie Rocco is a very good friend of mine. Two days ago my husband and I flew from Oregon to see her graduate at a university in Virginia. I also saw your wife, Julie, or I guess your soon-to-be ex-wife, graduate. After the graduation ceremony, my friend Stephanie's husband discovered that Julie had been murdered in her hotel room. Your mother-in-law said that her caregiver, Celia, was going to call you and tell you about Julie's murder. I certainly hope she did."

Mark sagged in his chair and put his head in his hands, then he looked up at Kelly, and with a catch in his voice said, "Yes, she called. I still can't believe it. You know, I never wanted the divorce. We were kind of like star-crossed lovers. She had her career, and I had this bed and breakfast, which is my career, and they weren't mutually compatible. Celia told me the police in Virginia have closed the file, since they believe a transient was responsible for Julie's murder."

"Yes, but I'm not so sure the transient really was the killer. My husband is a sheriff in Oregon, and he was at the graduation with me. He feels the chief of police took the easy way out. I've helped my husband solve several murder cases, and when Mrs. Logan learned that she asked for my help with this one."

"Why are you here?" he asked.

"I'm trying to get a sense of Julie and to understand why someone would want to murder her, although it very well may have been the transient."

"Julie was the most wonderful woman in the world. I don't think she had any enemies. Everyone loved her. She was beautiful and brilliant. I'll regret not doing more to save our marriage to my dying day."

"How did you handle living apart?" Kelly asked. "That must have been hard on both of you as well as expensive."

"It was. We decided when we got married we would each

continue to have our own separate bank account. In other words, she paid for her things, and I paid for mine. Unfortunately, things turned out a little different for us on that end. You see the bed and breakfast has been a real drain on my finances, actually almost to the point that I'm going to have to declare bankruptcy or sell it." He turned his hands up and said, "I don't know what else I can do. It all started when the economy took a real downturn two years ago, and I've never recovered from it."

"How did Julie feel about that?" Kelly asked.

"It happened about the time she decided our marriage wasn't going to work out. I know how wealthy Mrs. Logan is, but I never asked Julie if she would go to her mother and ask for financial help for me. You know, we Maine men are a proud and independent lot, and I'm certainly one of them. I would rather lose the bed and breakfast than have gone to Mrs. Logan on bended knee asking for a loan. No," he said shaking his head. "That was never an option."

"Have you kept in touch with Mrs. Logan?" she asked.

"Yes, we talk on the phone from time to time. I always liked her, and I think she likes me. Occasionally I'll stop by to say hi when I'm in Boston. She's a class act. As ill as she is, she never complains."

"Are you close to Julie's brother?"

"Are you serious? As if anyone could get close to him. I haven't seen him in over a year, but the last time I did, it wasn't a pleasant experience," Mark said in a harsh tone of voice.

"May I ask what happened?"

"Yes, he threatened me. He told me it was a good thing Julie and I were getting a divorce, so I'd never be able to get my hands on money that should be his. I guess he thought if Julie and I reconciled, she would inherit more money, and then I'd get some of it."

"I'm not really following that line of thinking," Kelly said.

"I'm not sure anyone could follow his line of thinking. I believe his heavy drinking over the years has had its effect on him. His thinking is simply not rational."

"Mark, you weren't divorced from Julie, right?"

"Yes, that's correct. The divorce was to become final next month, actually two days before my birthday on the 24th. I'll be forty-eight."

"Well, in that case, weren't you still her husband in the eyes of the law on the date of her death?"

He was quiet for a moment, then said, "I hadn't thought of it that way, but the answer must be yes. When I spoke with Celia, she indicated Mrs. Logan wanted to have Julie cremated and her ashes placed in the family crypt under the church they attended. I guess she realized we were still married and wanted my permission which I gave. At the time I was so shocked I never thought about why she was asking for my permission. As a strong Catholic, she was very opposed to us getting divorced. It's kind of a sick way to look at it, but at least Julie went to her death as a married woman, so the stigma of having both of her children divorced won't be an issue for Mrs. Logan."

"From what I saw, that's the least of her problems. Mark, I hate to bring this up, but did Julie ever mention to you she had a child out of wedlock right after she graduated from high school that she gave up for adoption?"

Mark stared at her, slack-jawed. "You're kidding, right?"

"No, I'm not." She told him how Megan had found Julie and about their having become reunited.

"I honestly don't know what to say. This is a complete shock to me. I'd like to meet her. Maybe there's a little of Julie in her."

"I hear she has Julie's red hair, and Julie told her mother Megan reminded her of what she was like at that age. I'm hoping to meet her when I return to Portland. I can certainly talk to her about you meeting with her. Let me ask you something else. Did you and Julie have wills?"

"Yes, after we were married we went to an attorney and had them drawn up. They were reciprocal wills. I left all of my estate to her, and she left everything to me. We talked about changing them if and when her mother died, because I didn't think it was fair for me to get that huge inheritance if Julie died first, although maybe it would have been better if I got it, rather than Clint. That would be a waste."

"Did you change your will after you and Julie separated?"

"Yes, I changed it and willed everything I own to my sister. She lives nearby, and even though she has three children, she's helped me out here at the bed and breakfast when I've been understaffed. Our parents are deceased, so she was my logical choice."

"Do you know if Julie changed her will?" Kelly asked.

"I have no idea. I've never thought about it. I assume she would have, but I can't say for sure."

"Mark, thank you for preventing whatever the intruder had planned. I enjoyed meeting you, and I hope you can find a way to keep this bed and breakfast open. It's charming, and the food at the restaurant was excellent."

He smiled for the first time that night. "I love this place. Believe me, if there's any way I can keep it open I will." He stood up and said, "I think you'll be fine for the rest of the night. I'm going to turn all of the cottage porchlights on. Here's my cell number. I'll keep my phone next to me, and if you hear anything tonight, just call me. See you in the morning. Come on, Max."

Kelly got down on one knee and petted the friendly yellow lab. "Nice meeting you, Max. Thanks." Max stood there for a moment, accepting the petting and wagging his tail.

Kelly got in bed and texted Stephanie. "Mark Jensen was born on June 22nd. He's forty-eight. You do the math. I'm brain dead. Don't bother to tell me the significance of any of their births. I'm on information overload. See you Thursday afternoon. Nite."

CHAPTER TWENTY-ONE

Kelly woke up surprisingly rested and refreshed given the scare she'd had during the night. She called the airline and made a reservation on a flight departing from Boston at one that afternoon. That would get her into Portland at about four, given the time change. She decided to wait and call Ryan and text Liz when she got to the airport, as it was too early on the West Coast for phone calls. She packed and then walked over to the main house for breakfast, promising herself she'd eat very little after last night.

"Good morning, Mrs. Reynolds, I trust you slept well."

"Very, Mark, thanks, and this looks delicious. What a spread!"

"People's breakfast eating habits vary, so I like them to have several options, although I can never pass up the banana bread. You might want to give it a try."

"Thanks, I will after I have a cup of coffee and just soak up the sights."

An hour later she put her suitcase in her rental car and walked back to the main house to check out. Mark was at the reception counter with Max next to him. "Checking out, Mrs. Reynolds?"

"Yes, I've thoroughly enjoyed my time in York, even with the excitement last night. It's simply beautiful here. Thanks again for helping me last night."

"I wouldn't be a very good host if I didn't do everything I could to make sure my guest's stays are both safe and enjoyable, and getting rid of an intruder certainly falls into the safe category. Mrs. Reynolds, I've been thinking about our conversation last night. I'd really like to meet Julie's daughter. Do you think I could?"

"I don't know why there would be a problem, but let me call you after I meet with her."

"Thanks. I'd appreciate anything you could do. Drive safely, and I hope to see you back here one of these days."

"Stranger things have happened in my life, Mark. You very well might!"

Kelly took the Interstate back to Boston and easily returned the rental car. She sat down on one of the benches across from the ticketing counter in the airport terminal and called Ryan.

"Hello, Kelly. How's the East Coast?" the male voice with the distinctive Irish lilt asked.

"Beautiful. I've had a lobster dinner and a lobster roll, so I guess it's time to return home. I'm getting into Portland about four this afternoon. I'm flying on American. Is there any chance you could pick me up and take me over to Julie's house? I'm sorry to ask you, but it would save me driving over to Cedar Bay tonight and then driving back to Portland tomorrow."

"Not a problem. By the way, I checked out your Facebook page, so I know what you look like. I'll be driving a grey SUV. I'll pick you up on the sidewalk outside the arrival level, next to the baggage claim."

"Thanks, Ryan, I really appreciate this. I'll text the person who was going to meet me that I'll be delayed. After we go to Julie's I'd like to go to the Heathman Hotel and see if I can meet Megan. Would you like to go with me? Might be appropriate, since you were her mother's attorney."

"Certainly, I have no plans this evening."

"Great, I'll see you about four on the sidewalk on the arrival level."

Next, she texted Liz and told her about the change of plans, asking her to confirm they were okay with her. A moment later her text notification buzzed. Liz told her to text her when she was ready to go to Cedar Bay and that she'd be waiting at a friend's home in Portland. Kelly looked at her watch and realized she had three hours to kill before her plane left. She picked up her cell phone and pressed in Mrs. Logan's number.

"This is Celia, Mrs. Reynolds. How can I help you?"

"Celia, you're just the one I wanted to talk to. How is Mrs. Logan doing today?"

"She's actually having a very good day. Would you like to talk to her?"

"Not really. I'm at the airport, and my flight doesn't leave for three hours. If it's not inconvenient, I thought I might visit her for a little while."

"That would be fine. I'm sure she would like to see you. I'll have Jasper pick you up. Where specifically are you?" she asked.

"I'll be outside in front of the American terminal on the departure level. Are you sure that's not an inconvenience for him?"

"Not at all. He's a driver and that's what drivers do, drive. We'll see you soon."

Twenty minutes later Kelly spotted the limousine and waved to

Jasper. He pulled up to the curb, and she quickly got in. "Thanks, Jasper, I really appreciate this. It's kind of spur of the moment."

After the short drive from the airport, Jasper pulled to a stop in front of the Logan mansion and walked around the car to open Kelly's door. "Mrs. Logan is having a good day. We're all keeping our fingers crossed hoping this new experimental drug is working. None of us want to see her in pain."

"Nor do I. Maybe it is a miracle drug. I'd like to believe it is, and with everything that's happened to her, I think she could use one."

The front door opened and Celia said, "Good morning, Mrs. Reynolds. Mrs. Logan is in the drawing room. She's looking forward to seeing you." She escorted Kelly into the room where she'd met Marcy Logan two days earlier.

"Hello, Marcy. I understand you're having a good day. I'm so glad," Kelly said as she put her hand on Mrs. Logan's frail shoulder.

"Yes, I'm beginning to hope this new drug is working, but I'm not sure that's a good thing or a bad thing."

"I think hope is always a good thing," Kelly answered. "I had some time before my flight back to Portland, and I wanted to stop by and bring you up to date." She proceeded to fill her in on Stephanie's suspicions about Sophie, her flying to Norfolk, and also told Mrs. Logan about her trip to York to meet Mark.

"You've been very busy, it seems," Mrs. Logan said in a faint and raspy voice. "Do you think someone other than the transient killed Julie?"

"I haven't found out anything definitive. When I return to Portland I'm meeting with Julie's attorney, and then we're going to her house to see if there's anything there that might shed some light on the mystery. After that I'd like to meet her daughter. Thursday afternoon I'm meeting with Sophie Marx and Stephanie."

"What did you think of Mark?" Mrs. Logan asked.

"I liked him a lot. He seemed devoted to Julie and is clearly shaken up by her sudden death. We talked about him being Julie's husband in the eyes of the law, since the divorce wouldn't have been final until next month. I don't think he'd really thought about it in that manner. Mark has made a new will and left everything he owns to his sister. He assumed Julie had also made a new will. Naturally, I never mentioned the fact that you'd given her ten million dollars, and that if she hadn't changed her will, then in that event, he would probably be the sole beneficiary of her estate which would include the ten million dollars."

"He was always special to me," Marcy said. "Even now he still stops by occasionally. I was heartsick when Julie decided to divorce him. I tried to tell her that marriage isn't quite like it's often portrayed in the movies, but I didn't have much luck. She was determined to begin a new life on the West Coast, and so she did. I do have a question. Do you think Megan could make a claim to Julie's estate, since she's Julie's biological daughter?"

"I don't know. That's definitely a question for a lawyer. I can ask Julie's lawyer when I meet with him this afternoon, if you'd like."

"Yes, I'm curious. This could get messy if that happens."

"I agree. Mrs. Logan, I need to ask you a couple of questions, and I'm concerned they might be painful for you."

"If it can help find out who murdered Julie, yes, please ask."

"Marcy, are you sure this is a good idea?" Celia asked standing next to her.

"Celia, maybe too many things went unsaid in this house, and it's time to right those wrongs." Her blue eyes looked steadily at Kelly. "Ask me what you will."

"Marcy, I had dinner with Clint the night before last night. He told me that he no longer drinks, that he got a job at your insurance company, and that he had gone to Julie's graduation intending to speak with her and attempt to make amends with her. Did you know about any of this?"

Mrs. Logan looked down at her hands for a long time and then looked up at Kelly, her eyes bright with unshed tears. "Kelly, I don't know about the graduation and the drinking, but I do know he's not employed by the insurance company."

Celia audibly gasped and exclaimed in a shrill voice, "Why Marcy, how can that be? He sat right here in this room and told you he'd taken a job there. Did you call the company?"

"It's not an easy thing to admit you raised a son who is a bald-faced liar, especially a son who would lie to his own mother. I knew he thought I was too old and too ill to check it out, but I called my husband's old secretary. She's about ready to retire, and we talk from time to time. I told her what Clint had said about working for the company, and she told me she was wasn't aware of him working there, but she said she'd call Human Resources and find out for sure. She called me back yesterday afternoon and told me there was no record of him currently working for the company."

"Marcy, I'm so sorry. I'm afraid I have some other bad news for you." She told Marcy about her conversation with the hostess at the restaurant. "Since he seems to have lied about working for the insurance company, and a reliable source told me he hasn't stopped drinking, I'm wondering what to believe about him claiming he attended Julie's graduation."

"I have no idea what to tell you."

"Did you tell him that Julie had been reunited with her daughter, and that she has red hair?"

"No. I knew it would only make him angry, and he would be concerned that it might cut into his inheritance."

"Do you have any idea how he would know, if he did?"

The three of them were quiet for a few moments and then Celia spoke. "Marcy, I hate to say this, and I don't want to accuse Clint of anything, but one time when he was here at the house I happened to come down from your room unexpectedly. He was standing over there where the phone jack is located. The only reason I bring it up is I was watching a show on television the other night after you'd gone to bed, and a person in the show had installed a bug on the phone jack that allowed him to hear conversations between people. I wonder if Clint might have done something like that."

Mrs. Logan was quiet for a moment and then she said with steely determination, "Call Jonathan and have him come over and see if he can find anything." She turned to Kelly and said, "He's the electrician we've used for years when we've had telephone or electrical problems here at the hose. He knows everything about this house, because he upgraded everything several years ago. Celia, I want you to call him right now."

"Yes, ma'am," Celia said. She returned a few minutes later. "Jonathan will be here as soon as he finishes the job he's on. He says it should be within the next two hours."

"I'm so sorry to bring all of this up. I know it has to be painful for you," Kelly said.

"It's terribly painful, but I want to get to the bottom of this. If, in fact, Clint had something to do with Julie's murder, I don't know if I can ever forgive myself for allowing it to happen."

"Mrs. Logan, I'm not a psychologist, but it seems to me Clint had the same opportunities and the same parents that Julie did. Some people turn out differently for whatever reason. You can't blame yourself for Clint's actions."

"Thank you, but I can't help blaming myself for the way he's turned out. If anyone is responsible, I suppose it would be me. It sure doesn't look like he's going to claim any responsibility."

"That may be true, but I really think we all do the best we can do at any given time. If we could do something else, we probably would. We still don't know if any of our thoughts regarding Clint are true. I need to get to the airport. Celia, could you call Jasper for me?"

"Of course." She walked over to the house phone, made a call, and said, "He'll be in front of the house in five minutes."

Kelly walked over to where Mrs. Logan was seated and said, "Marcy, no matter what we find out, you can't blame yourself. I think anyone would be honored to have you for a mother or a grandmother. Maybe getting to know the granddaughter you became separated from all those years ago would be a good idea. I'll call you when I know something. I'd appreciate it if you'd let me know what Jonathan finds out about your phone possibly being bugged. I feel honored to have met you. Thank you, and I'm praying for a miracle for you."

She walked to the front door and turned to Celia who had accompanied her. "I assume you're going to take her up to her room, so she can rest for a while."

"Yes, she likes to think she's strong, but this is definitely taking its toll on her."

"Celia, may I have your cell phone number? If I find out anything disturbing, maybe the two of us should be in agreement about how much I should tell her."

"That would be a good idea, and thanks for being so sensitive to this difficult situation."

"Goodbye, Celia. Take care of her."

"Trust me, Mrs. Reynolds, that's one thing you definitely don't need to worry about."

Less than a half hour later Jasper pulled up to the American departure level and said, "Have a safe flight, Mrs. Reynolds. I look forward to seeing you again."

Kelly stepped out of the limousine, waved goodbye to him, and walked into the busy terminal, pulling her roller bag behind her.

CHAPTER TWENTY-TWO

The plane trip back to Portland was uneventful. Kelly spent the time alternating between looking out the window, trying to solve in her mind the mystery surrounding the murder of Julie Jensen, and reading the novel she'd brought with her. After they landed she retrieved her bag from the baggage carousel and walked out to the curb. Within minutes a grey SUV pulled up, and the driver waved to her. He opened the passenger window and said, "Hi Kelly. I'm Ryan. I'd get out and open the door for you, but in this traffic that probably isn't a very good idea."

She quickly got in his SUV and said, "Thanks so much for meeting me. It's been an eventful couple of days. Excuse me for a moment. I need to check my messages after that long flight. Looks like I've got two of them. I'll just be a minute."

Both voicemail messages were from numbers she didn't recognize. Kelly listened to the first one and gasped. Ryan turned towards her, an inquisitive look on his face. She held her hand up in a gesture indicating she was still listening. After she listened to the second message, she sat back against the seat and closed her eyes, clearly stunned at what she'd just heard.

"Kelly do you want to share the messages or are they something personal?"

She opened her eyes and said, "Ryan, I don't know what to make of them, but I'm concerned. First let me fill you in on a couple of things." She told him about her dinner with Clint and Celia's suspicion that he might have installed a phone tap on Mrs. Logan's phone.

She continued, "The first message was from Jasper, who is Julie's mother's driver. After he took me to the airport around noon today he got a call from Clint asking Jasper to pick him up and take him to a nearby private airport. Jasper said Clint did that from time to time, and Mrs. Logan didn't mind. Evidently Clint had hired a private plane. Jasper said he'd been drinking heavily, but what was frightening to Jasper was that Clint had shaved off his goatee and all of his hair. His bright red hair and bright red goatee were completely gone, according to Jasper. He'd even shaved his eyebrows.

"He said there was absolutely no trace of his trademark red hair. Jasper said it was just weird. He asked Clint where he was going, but Clint wouldn't tell him. The only thing he said was 'that he needed to take care of a business matter.' Jasper couldn't figure out what kind of business he needed to take care of, because as far as he knew, Clint had never had any business dealings. He told Mrs. Logan's caregiver about it, and both of them thought I should know about it. He said he wasn't going to tell Mrs. Logan."

"I agree it's certainly unusual behavior, but I fail to see what it has to do with Julie's death."

"Me neither, but for some reason it makes me nervous. The second message was from Celia, Mrs. Logan's caregiver. She said Jonathan, the electrician the Logan family has used for years, had searched the drawing room for an electronic telephone bug. He found one that had been put on the phone jack. He said whoever put it there was able to monitor all conversations that took place on the house phone. If it was Clint, it would certainly explain how he knew Julie and her daughter had reunited and that Megan had red hair. He probably also knew that Mrs. Logan had given Julie a gift of ten million dollars.

"I honestly don't know what to think, Ryan, but it seems to me I should move Clint up to the top of the suspect list. The problem is, I have no idea how I or anyone else can prove he's the murderer." She sighed deeply. "By the way, I have a legal question to ask you."

"Go ahead. Ask your question, and I'll help you if I can, but first I want to talk to you about Julie's will. I got it from the bank vault and just as we thought, she hadn't changed it. Under the terms of the will her husband, Mark Jensen, is to receive distribution of her entire estate. Kind of ironic, given the fact they were going to get divorced, and she'd made an appointment with me to prepare a new will, but the law's the law. According to her will Mark's entitled to the ten million dollars Julie's mother gave her last week. Wow, what a strange turn of events. Sorry, Kelly, I'm rambling. What did you want to ask me?"

"If Megan can prove she's Julie's daughter, and I have no reason to think she wouldn't be able to, could she sue her mother's estate claiming that she's Julie's rightful heir?"

Ryan was quiet for a few moments while he thought about Kelly's question. "You know that anyone can sue for any reason, but I don't see her doing it for two reasons. She's an adoption attorney, and she, above all people, would know that when a parent gives a child up for adoption, that means the child is entitled to nothing further from their biological parent. In other words, the cord is completely severed. Secondly, while she could sue, Julie's will clearly states that her husband is to receive her entire estate. A child given up for adoption would have no valid claim to that money. The terms of Julie's will trump the inheritance rights of an heir. If Julie didn't have a will, that might be a different story. Ahh, there's her house now."

Ryan parked the SUV in the driveway, while Kelly looked out the window at the house. "Ryan, this is charming. Her house must be a hundred years old. The green shutters are a perfect accent to the white paint and the white picket fence. It looks like something out of a storybook right down to the trees in bloom and the shrubbery. With the riot of color around the house, she must have planted hundreds of bulbs last fall. If her house is any indication of what she was like, I have a feeling I really would have liked her."

They got out of his SUV and walked over to the steps leading up to the front door which had a spring wreath displayed on it. "Kelly, what are you looking for? Anything specific? What would you like me to do?" Ryan asked.

"Well, I'm not looking for anything specific. Now that you have the will, that's not an issue anymore. I just hope to run across something that will help me figure out this case. What I think we should do to maximize our time is for each of us to take one room at a time and see if we can find anything." Ryan unlocked the door and they walked into the house and started looking around.

"Why don't you take the living room and dining room? I'll take her bedroom and her office," Kelly said. "Once those four rooms are done, we can decide what else we need to do. I think we can rule out the garage. It's been my experience that garages are more of a male domain, so I'd really be surprised if there was anything of interest to us in it."

"Sounds good to me," Ryan said, as he walked into the living room. Kelly heard the sound of drawers being opened as he began his search. She walked down the hall looking in the bedrooms. At the end of the hall was a large bedroom with French doors which opened out onto a large grassy expanse and contained more trees and flowers.

CHAPTER TWENTY-THREE

I know I would have liked her, Kelly thought, as she walked into what she assumed had been Julie's bedroom. *It's just as charming as the outside of the house. Feminine, but not cutesy-poosey, if that's even a word. Think I'll start with the nightstand.*

Kelly opened the nightstand drawer and gasped when she saw a small pistol in it. *Why would Julie feel she had to sleep with a gun next to her? I wonder if she'd been threatened.* She checked the gun and made sure the safety was on and then took it out of the drawer. Thirty minutes later she was certain there was nothing in the bedroom that would help resolve her unanswered questions about Julie's murder.

She walked down the hall to a room that was clearly being used as an office. A large brightly colored Oriental rug was positioned in the center of the room, covering the highly polished wood floor. Against one wall was an antique roll top oak desk. Across from it was an upholstered couch repeating the bright reds, blues, creams, and lilacs of the Oriental rug. Kelly looked in the drawer of the small table that was positioned between the couch and a large chair with an ottoman and found nothing. On the table was a pile of books. She leafed through them and again found nothing. Bookcases flanked the floor to ceiling French windows which looked out on hanging flower baskets attached to a small patio overhang. The baskets were filled with brightly colored trailing plants.

As she was carefully examining each shelf, a book caught her eye entitled "The Logan Family History." It had been written by Marcy Logan and carefully documented the original Logan family members who had come to the United States from Scotland during the Colonial period. Composed of nearly three hundred fifty pages, the book was rather large and heavy. It was filled with photographs of the people mentioned in the book. Kelly put it on the couch, intending to give it to Megan. *Actually*, she thought, *there's really no one else. It doesn't seem to be the kind of thing Clint would like, and since I have serious concerns about him, I'm definitely going to give it to Megan.*

She sat down at the desk and booted up Julie's computer. Evidently Julie wasn't concerned about someone hacking her computer, because it wasn't password protected, or if it was, she hadn't bothered to use it. Kelly went through emails, files, the last web sites Julie had visited, and anything else she thought might provide some information or help. She found nothing. After she decided it was a dead end, she opened a small drawer on the right hand side of the desk. Julie had carefully stacked various bills and receipts in the drawer. Kelly glanced through them and found nothing of interest.

Kelly pulled the drawer out as far it would go and saw a checkbook in the back. She opened it and looked at the check register which recorded the checks written and deposits made for the last month. There was nothing out of the ordinary except the ten-million-dollar deposit which had been noted.

She continued her search of the other desk drawers, finding labeled manila folders for things like household maintenance, insurance, etc., but nothing of interest. As she was preparing to leave the room, something about the checkbook nagged her. She took it out of the drawer again and noticed that the packet containing a supply of blank deposit slips had been inserted at an extremely odd angle, and as much of a perfectionist as Julie seemed to have been, Kelly thought she would have made sure the edges were evenly aligned. She pulled the deposit packet out of the checkbook's plastic holder and gingerly stuck her finger into the empty slot. She felt a piece of paper and pulled it out. A look of shock crossed her face as she read the words written on the paper, "You'll never live to spend the ten million dollars."

She dropped it on the desk and called out, "Hey, Ryan, would you mind coming back here to the office? I've found something."

A moment later Ryan entered the room. "Kelly, are you all right? You're as white as a ghost. What did you find?"

She wordlessly handed the piece of paper to him, watching his expression as he read it. He put it down on the desk and said, "That's pretty ominous. What do you think?"

"The same thing I'm sure you're thinking. I read it as a threat. Actually it's more than just a threat, it's a death threat, and it certainly explains why I found a loaded pistol in the drawer of Julie's nightstand."

"Do you think she knew who sent it? I wonder if it was hand-delivered or mailed to her."

"I have no idea," Kelly said. "This is all I found, and it was wedged behind the deposit packet in her checkbook. That doesn't seem like a random place to put something. There's nothing to indicate when, or how, or even where it was received by her. According to her checkbook records she received the ten million dollars a week before she was to graduate. Her mother told me it was a graduation present."

"What do you want to do now? I don't think there's any point in calling the authorities, do you? Since the murder happened in Virginia, I suppose you could call the police chief there, but from what you told me, it doesn't sound like he'd do much with this kind of information."

"I don't think there's anything we can do about it, but I'm going to take it with me. I guess Mark will get this house too, am I right?" Kelly asked.

"Yes, it's obviously part of her estate."

"I think I'll take the gun with me as well as this paper and a book I found about the Logan family history. I'm uncomfortable leaving a gun in a house when someone's been murdered. I'll take it home and give it my husband. I'm sure sheriffs have ways to dispose of unwanted guns."

"Kelly, it's already six-thirty. You mentioned you wanted to try and see Megan tonight. Why don't you give her a call? If we spend an hour or so there, you're going to get home pretty late, and I imagine your husband will be getting concerned."

"Ryan," she grinned, "you don't know the half of it. My husband is always concerned when I'm involved in anything, particularly if it's a murder investigation. I also have to admit his concern is often with good reason. I do have a way of getting into, how shall I put it, some interesting situations."

She took her phone out of her purse and got the number for the Heathman Hotel. A moment later she heard a voice inquire, "How may I direct your call?"

"I believe you have a guest staying there by the name of Megan Simmons. Would you connect me to her room? Thank you."

Kelly had an old habit of crossing her fingers behind her back if she was on iffy ground with Mike. The gesture came naturally to her, and she found she was crossing her fingers, hoping Megan was there and would agree to see her.

"Hello," a soft female voice said.

"Is this Megan Simmons?" Kelly asked.

"Yes. Who's calling?"

"Megan, my name is Kelly Reynolds. You don't know me, but I'm a very good friend of Stephanie Rocco. Your mother worked for her here in Portland. I went to Virginia last Saturday to see her receive a graduate degree from a university in Virginia, and I saw your mother graduate as well. I have something for you, and I'm hoping I can meet with you at your hotel in a few minutes."

"That sounds interesting. I haven't heard from my mother for a few days, and I was going to call her later. If you have something for me, I'll wait and tell her about it. I'm in room 507. When will you be here?"

Kelly looked over at Ryan who indicated they could be there in fifteen minutes. "I should be there in about fifteen minutes. I'm looking forward to meeting you," she said with a sinking heart, knowing she was going to have to be the one to tell Megan that the mother she had just found had been murdered. "Let's go, Ryan, I'm not looking forward to this, but I didn't want to tell her over the phone."

CHAPTER TWENTY-FOUR

Due to heavy downtown traffic Ryan was off by five minutes in his fifteen minute travel time estimate for how long it would take them to get to Megan's hotel. He drove up to the hotel entrance, stopped, and handed the car keys to the valet. A second valet held the door open for them. "Ryan, this is a beautiful hotel. The chandeliers and the wood are incredible. No wonder it's considered to be one of Portland's finest."

"Yes, if it's not the best hotel in Portland, it's right up there. I've often met clients here and have never been disappointed in anything dealing with it." They walked through the lobby to the bank of elevators. Ryan turned to Kelly and said, "I need to use the men's room before I go up to Megan's room. It's 507 right? I'll just be a few minutes."

"Yes, it's 507. Take your time. I'll meet you there."

Kelly rode the elevator up to the fifth floor and stepped out. The sign on the wall across from the elevator indicated that room 507 was to the left. She looked at the room numbers on the doors and realized it was at the far end of the hall. A few moments later she knocked on the door to room 507.

"Who is it?" a voice asked. Although the voice sounded similar to Megan's voice on the phone a short while ago, this one seemed to be tense, almost teary. *What is this all about*, Kelly wondered.

"Megan, it's Kelly Reynolds. I spoke to you a few minutes ago."

The door opened, and Kelly looked at the woman in front of her who had a terror stricken look on her face. "Come in," she stammered tremulously. Kelly walked in and suddenly a hand reached out from behind Megan and slammed the door. Kelly whirled around and the first thing she was a gun pointing at her chest. She raised her eyes and saw that the gun was being held by Clint Logan.

"Glad you called, Kelly. You saved me a lot of trouble. I tried to take care of you in York, but that stupid brother-in-law of mine and his dumb dog wouldn't let me. Too bad. I just told my niece that her mother isn't around anymore.

"You see, I had to kill Julie to make sure I got all of Mother's money when she died, not just some of it. I've always hated my sister and all the special treatment she got from my mother and father. When I listened to the phone tap I put on her phone and found out she'd given Julie ten million dollars, it put me over the edge.

"I knew I had to act, and I had to act fast before the old biddy died, so I hopped on a plane to Norfolk, found Julie in her hotel room and shot her. I planted her wallet, jewelry, and the pistol I'd used to kill Julie on some drunken bum I saw in the parking lot as I was leaving. I slugged him on the head as hard as I could with an iron bar I found by a broken gate. I made it look like he'd fallen and suffered a skull fracture. Sort of ironic, one drunk kills another one. The whole package turned out nice and neat, and according to the local paper I read, the police chief says the case is closed.

"Since Megan's the only other person that can lay claim to Mother's estate, I thought it might be a good idea to get rid of her before Mother decides to leave Julie's share to her. You can both sit down for a moment. It's a shame I'm going to have to kill my niece when I've just met her, but I don't have much choice, and I don't have much time. I told the pilot that flew me out here this wouldn't take long, and it won't."

He looked directly at Megan and said in a slurred voice, "You got the Logan red hair, that's for sure. You look just like your mother did when she was your age. Good thing I shaved my head and beard. No one here at the hotel will associate me with the redhead I'll be in a couple of weeks or so. And who would even think I'd come to Portland in the first place? No one. Either of you got any last words you want to say, because it's about time," he said as he raised the gun and pointed it at Kelly's head with a crazy and wild look in his eyes.

Just then there was a knock on the door. "Who are you expecting?" he hissed.

"No one," Megan replied.

"Go to the door and look through the peephole," he said.

"It's a friend of mine that came with me," Kelly said. "He went to the restroom. He knows I'm in here."

"Then Kelly, you go to the door instead of Megan and let him in. I wasn't planning on anything but Megan's death, but now I guess it will have to be all three of you."

Kelly walked over to the door as Clint stepped to a position where he would be hidden behind the door once Kelly opened it, but his gun swung menacingly back and forth between Kelly and Megan. She opened the door and saw Ryan standing there. The only thing she could think to do that Clint couldn't see from his position behind the door was to blink rapidly with her eyes.

"Come in, Ryan," she said, continuing to rapidly blink as she stepped away from the door. She saw Ryan's hand go to his waist as his other hand violently pushed the door back as forcibly as he could, catching Clint off guard and causing him to lose his balance in his drunken condition and drop his gun. Kelly reached for the Logan Family History book and threw it at Clint, hitting him squarely on the side of his head with the heavy book. It seemed everyone in the room was in a flurry of motion. Ryan drew a gun from a holster attached to his belt, while Megan picked up Clint's gun. Kelly reached over and took it from her trembling hands.

"Don't move, mister," Ryan shouted in a loud commanding voice. "You've got two guns on you, and as soon as the police get here, there will be more. Stretch your hands out in front of you. I want to see them. I'm calling the police chief. I play golf with him, and he happens to be a friend of mine."

Within minutes the room was filled with men and women in blue uniforms. Clint was handcuffed and taken away by two policemen. As he left, Kelly heard him say, "I demand to call Mother. You have no idea who you are dealing with. I'm Clint Logan of the Boston Logans. My mother will have her lawyer get me out on bail as soon as I make the call."

The burly policeman who was behind him said, "Don' think so, pal. Judges take a real dim view around here of people who are charged with three counts of attempted murder, plus the three people in the hotel room tell us you also admitted to a double homicide back in Virginia. Don't think being a Boston Logan will do you a bit of good. Know there's a Logan airport in Boston, and even if it was named after your family, still wouldn't help you here. Pal, you're toast, and you're gonna be toast for a long time."

The hotel corridor was filled with curious guests and onlookers. For the next hour Kelly, Megan, and Ryan told the police chief and his detectives what had happened. Kelly gave the piece of paper with the threat on it to the police chief. When the last one had left, Kelly turned to Megan and said, "How are you doing? You've been through so much in your life, and now this. I wanted to be the one to tell you about your mother and do it in a kinder and gentler way. I'm so sorry it didn't happen that way."

"I don't know what to think," Megan said as tears stared to roll down her cheeks. "I've never been happier than when my mother and I were reunited, and now this. It's as if something precious was given to me and then brutally ripped away."

"Megan, why don't you come home with me tonight?" Kelly said.

"I live in Cedar Bay which is about two hours from here. I don't think it's a good idea for you to be by yourself tonight. A friend of mine is picking me up, and I have three dogs who would like to do nothing more than make you feel good. You can call court tomorrow and tell them you've had a family emergency, but I think you need a little time to let all of this settle in."

"Thank you. That's really kind of you. Actually the judge who's in charge of the trial I had scheduled for tomorrow and Friday had a family emergency and canceled all of her cases for the next two days. If you're sure it wouldn't be an imposition, I think I'd like some company. Let me pack my things, and I'll check out."

"Kelly, I'll check out for Megan. You stay here with her. I'll see you downstairs in a few minutes," Ryan said.

"Wait a minute, Ryan. Do you always carry a gun?"

He smiled sheepishly and said, "No. I had a call last night from a man named Sheriff Mike Reynolds. Think you know him. Anyway, he said you had a tendency to get into dangerous situations, and he'd feel a lot better knowing I was carrying a gun when I was with you. It's a good thing I had it because we sure didn't know when we put Julie's gun in the trunk of my car that we'd need one."

"Well, he promised he wouldn't make that call, but under the circumstances, I'm glad he did."

"Me too, and I think it was kind of fitting that the book you threw at Clint was the Logan Family History. Sort of karmic justice," he said with a smile on his face as he opened the door and walked out.

While Megan was packing, Kelly texted Liz who said she was on her way and she also texted Mike saying the case was solved, and she was bringing Julie's daughter, Megan, home with her. She told him she'd give him all the details when she got home.

CHAPTER TWENTY-FIVE

Liz pulled into the driveway and immediately the front door opened and Rebel, Lady, and Skyy raced out to greet Kelly, followed by Mike who put his arms around Kelly and kissed her. He stepped back, looked at Megan and said, "You must be Megan. Excuse the dogs. They're just a little excited at the moment. I'm Mike, Kelly's husband. Welcome to Cedar Bay. The boxer is Rebel, the yellow lab is Lady, and the German shepherd who's running around in circles and still has a lot of puppy in her is Skyy. Let me get your bag."

"Thanks, Liz," Kelly said. "I really appreciate you driving over to Portland to pick me up. I promise I'll return the favor. Say hi to Doc for me." Kelly had been responsible for Doc starting a new life in Cedar Bay and Liz, his wife, was part of that happy story. Although it had been several years earlier, they were still close, and Doc remained one of the regular lunchtime customers at Kelly's Koffee Shop.

Kelly, Megan, and Mike walked into the house followed by three very happy dogs. Having Kelly back was great, but even better was having a new person around they hoped they could get to play with them. Since belly rubs were their favorite thing, they were sure this stranger would know what to do when they rolled over on their backs.

Mike walked down the hall and said, "Megan, here's the guest bedroom. There's an attached bathroom. Let us know if you need anything. I don't know what happened tonight, but it looks like you could use a good night's sleep. The good news is the dogs would love to make a new friend. The bad news is they will probably be in your room until you shoo them out and close the door, and please, feel free to do so."

"Kelly, Mike, thank you so much for letting me stay with you. I really am tired. I think I'd like to go to bed. I hope the dogs understand. I promise I'll give them some attention in the morning."

"Megan, you do whatever feels good to you," Kelly said. "Feel free to sleep in. We'll both be around in the morning. I've already arranged for someone to handle my coffee shop. I don't have to go back to work until next week. Let me get you some fresh towels for you."

She started down the hall to the linen closet when Mike stopped her. "I decided to be a good host, and I've already done that. I don't know what happened, but I think you probably need a little rest as well. You look tired and ought to head off to bed, but first let's go into the other room, and you can tell me everything."

"Mike, you have no idea how good it is to be home. That poor young woman. She found her mother and only a couple of weeks later, she loses her mother. By the way, thanks for calling Ryan. He saved our lives."

"Well now, isn't that just swell? How can you offhandedly say someone saved your life? If I played a part in that, I'm glad, but I would like to hear exactly how he saved your life and what led up to it."

Kelly spent the next hour telling Mike everything that had happened from the time she'd ended her call to him the evening before to Clint's arrest and then her trip to Cedar Bay with Megan and Liz. When she was finished she said, "So, Mike, what do you think?"

"I think Megan was very lucky you happened to call her, and I think you and Megan were very lucky I happened to call Ryan. There is one thing that's concerning me."

"What?" Kelly asked, as she stretched and yawned, the climactic events of the day starting to catch up with her.

"You didn't say anything about Mrs. Logan. Do you know if she's been told that Clint's in custody? If he's called her, I can't believe that kind of news would be good for someone in her condition."

"Mike, with everything that's happened in the last few hours, no, I didn't even think to call her. I wonder if she knows. It's late back there with the time difference, but I think I'll send a long text to Celia about everything that's happened. At least if Mrs. Logan has been told, Celia will have the facts."

"I think that's a good idea, and I have another idea which you may not like."

"If you say it that way, I probably won't, but go ahead, shoot," Kelly said.

"I think when you text Celia you should tell her that you and Megan are flying to Boston tomorrow. Lower your eyebrows, Kelly, and let me finish. Anyway, Clint and Megan are her only relatives that we know of, and I imagine Clint is going to be spending a long time in prison, either here in Oregon or in Virginia, depending on what the prosecuting attorneys decide to do about the charges pending against him.

"I think you should tell Mrs. Logan in person about Clint and also introduce her to Megan, the granddaughter she's never met. Think about it while I let the dogs out."

He returned a few minutes later, and said, "Well?"

"As much as I don't want to do it, I probably should. I'll ask Celia if it would be all right for us to come and tell her to make a reservation for us at the Parker House for tomorrow night. I can fly back Friday, and Megan can decide what she wants to do after she meets with Mrs. Logan."

"I think that's a good idea, but if I were you, I'd make the travel arrangements now. Celia's probably in bed and won't look at your text until tomorrow morning. If she says it's not a good idea to come, all you have to do is cancel the reservations."

"Do you think I should ask Megan if she even wants to go? Maybe she'd like to forget about the whole family thing."

"I don't think you should wake her, and as strongly as she pursued finding her mother, I can't believe she wouldn't want to meet her grandmother, particularly, since other than her uncle Clint, that's her only other biological relative. If for some reason it turns out she doesn't want to go, at least you'll have your reservation, but I do think you owe it to Mrs. Logan to tell her exactly what happened. I'm sure the story she'll get from Clint will be much different. My schedule at work is clear for tomorrow morning, so I can take you to Portland. See if you can get an early flight."

"Okay. I'll get started. Why don't you go on to bed? I'll be there as soon as I make the flight reservations and text Celia. Oh, there's one other thing I need to do."

"What's that?"

"I need to text Stephanie and tell her what happened. She was going to schedule a meeting with Sophie tomorrow afternoon and find out why she went to Norfolk. I was going to meet with them. Guess that's unnecessary now, but I am curious why she went."

"Okay, I'm off to bed. Welcome home," Mike said as he walked down the hall.

CHAPTER TWENTY-SIX

Kelly's text message alert went off at 5:00 the next morning. She reached over and read the message Celia had written.

"Yes, please come and bring Megan. With her health issues, Marcy has been concerned she'd never have the chance to meet her granddaughter. Clint called last night and told Mrs. Logan to hire an attorney for him. He said there had been a misunderstanding. She said she wanted to talk to you first and told me he sounded really strange. She was planning on calling you this morning. I think I need to read her your text before you get here. At least she'll have a chance to absorb what has happened, and knowing that her granddaughter is coming to meet her will probably help boost her spirits. Text me with your flight arrangements, and I'll have Jasper pick you up at the airport, and forget about the Parker House. We have more empty bedrooms in this house than we know what to do with."

Kelly texted her back with their flight arrival information and went into the kitchen to make a pot of coffee. The flight she'd made reservations on left Portland at 8:00 a.m., so there wasn't much time to spare. Getting dressed, packed, and grabbing a cup of coffee for the drive would take up the next forty-five minutes.

She knocked on Megan's door and opened it. "Megan, I'm sorry to wake you, but I need to talk to you," Kelly said.

"What is it?" Megan asked groggily.

"Since you said you were free the next few days, I took the liberty of making plane reservations for us to go to Boston. I've been in touch with your grandmother's caregiver, and I want to tell your grandmother what happened with Clint in person. Her caregiver told me your grandmother is very anxious to meet you. Given her state of health, I feel time is of the essence. We really don't have much time. Our flight leaves Portland at 8:00 this morning. Mike will drive us to the airport. You need to get dressed and packed. Coffee will be ready in a few minutes. Is there anything you need?"

"No, not really," Megan said, now very much awake. "I can't believe I'm going to meet my grandmother. Are you sure it's a good idea?"

"Absolutely. If it wasn't, I never would have made the reservations, and I probably couldn't live with myself if I didn't tell your grandmother about Clint in person. See you in a few minutes."

Kelly walked back into the master bedroom, bent over and gave a sleeping Mike a kiss. He opened his eyes and smiled at her. "Mike, it's kind of like that fairy tale. When I kissed you, you woke up. Remember which one it was?"

"I think it was Sleeping Beauty, but don't quote me. Do you have to sound so chipper this early? The sun isn't even up yet."

"I heard from Celia, and the trip is a go. Megan's getting ready, and we need to leave in about half an hour. I made coffee. You need to roll out of bed and get ready to drive us to the airport. Sorry to desert you again, but you were right, I do need to tell Mrs. Logan in person everything that's happened."

"Kelly, I just thought of something. I wonder when Ryan is planning on telling Mark about his windfall. Do you know if he even has Mark's contact information?"

"No. Let me text him. Since I know Mark, maybe I should be the one to tell him." She quickly texted Ryan and received an answer a few minutes later just as she stepped out of the shower. "He must get up early," she said. "Mike, he asked if I would tell Mark he's to receive Julie's entire estate including the house and the ten million dollars. When I return from Boston I'm to give him Mark's contact information, and he'll take care of all the legal probate details. Wow! What a day this is going to be."

"What are you doing now?" Mike asked as he watched her hurriedly typing on her cell phone.

"I texted Mark and asked him if he could meet me at Mrs. Logan's around seven this evening. I told him it was very important. Ahh, he's already texted me back and said yes. Hurry, you need to get dressed."

The three of them left the house at five forty-five and easily drove to the airport in far less time than it usually took. Of course, being in a black and white sheriff's patrol car with the red lights activated and the siren blaring probably helped.

"Ladies, I'm going to drop you off rather than go in with you. I need to get back to Cedar Bay, but I'll sure be thinking about you today and tonight," Mike said. He took their luggage out of the trunk, kissed Kelly warmly and then kissed Megan on the cheek. "Be safe. Kelly, I'll see you tomorrow and Megan, I hope it won't be long before I see you again, too. Goodbye and good luck." He got back in his patrol car and slowly pulled into traffic.

"Well, Megan," Kelly said as they walked into the terminal, "It's going to be interesting to see what this day brings."

CHAPTER TWENTY-SEVEN

Kelly and Megan landed at Logan Airport in Boston at 4:30 in the afternoon, local time. They easily retrieved their luggage from the baggage carousel and walked towards the door. As soon as Kelly opened the door she saw Jasper standing next to the black limousine, waiting for them.

"Jasper, thank you so much for picking us up. Megan, I want you to meet Jasper, your grandmother's driver. Jasper, this is Megan, Julie's daughter."

For a moment Jasper stood perfectly still, seemingly dumbstruck as he looked at Megan. Then he said, "I'm sorry for staring, Miss Megan, but I feel like I'm looking at Miss Julie. You're the spitting image of your mother. I'll get your luggage and put it in the trunk," he said as he opened the limousine's rear door for them.

Twenty minutes later the limousine pulled up in front of the Logan mansion. Megan stared at it, wide-eyed. Kelly thought she saw a drape in one of the windows pulled back slightly and wondered if Mrs. Logan or Celia had been looking out the window watching for them.

Kelly glanced at Megan and saw how nervous she was. She reached over and put her hand on Megan's arm. "Just relax, it's going to be fine. Trust me. Your grandmother is a lovely woman."

Before Kelly and Megan could knock on the front door, it was opened by Celia. She hugged Kelly and looked at Megan. "Of course you're Julie's daughter. I'd know you anywhere. Come, I need a hug from you, too." They walked into the hallway and Celia said, "Your grandmother is in the drawing room. I must tell you, Megan, she's very nervous about meeting you."

"You're kidding. You think she's nervous! I've never been so nervous in my life. What if she doesn't like me or something?"

"Trust me. She's been waiting for this moment for a long time, although with everything that's happened, it's rather bittersweet."

They entered the drawing room, and Kelly saw Marcy's small frame seated in a chair at the far end of the room. Her piercing blue eyes took everything in, and in a strong voice she said, "Child, please come here. I want to see my granddaughter."

Kelly and Celia hung back as Megan slowly walked over to her grandmother. They looked at each other for a moment and it was very apparent to both Kelly and Celia that each of them was struggling to hold back their emotions. Finally, Mrs. Logan said, "Child, it's customary in Boston for grandchildren to give their grandmother a hug and a kiss. Please, won't you come here?" Tears ran down Megan's face as she embraced her grandmother who was also crying. Kelly didn't realize she was crying until Celia handed her a handkerchief. Several long moments went by and no one spoke. Megan and Marcy simply clasped hands, smiled at each other, and continued crying.

Celia broke the mood and said, "Megan, why don't you sit down in the chair next to Marcy? Kelly, you can sit in the chair over there. Marcy, ladies, may I bring you something?"

"I'd like you to take a bottle of champagne out of the wine cooler. It's been a long time since this house has had something to celebrate, but tonight we will celebrate." She turned to Kelly. "Please tell me everything. All I know is Clint called and asked me to get an attorney for him, that he was being framed for something he didn't do."

"Wait, Marcy. Before Kelly starts, I think a toast would be in order and I'd like to make it," Celia said as she filled the crystal champagne flutes. "It a very simple toast, but given the circumstances, one I think is most appropriate." She held her glass up and said, "To new beginnings." They lightly touched the other's glasses and took a sip of the Dom Perignon champagne.

"Well, this is a first," Kelly said. "I've heard the name, but I've never tasted Dom Perignon champagne before. It's delicious, but it sets an awfully high benchmark."

"That's what comes with being a Boston Brahmin. You develop expensive tastes and habits," Marcy said, laughing.

"What's a Boston Brahmin?" Kelly asked.

"I think it was Oliver Wendell Holmes who coined the phrase in the late 19th century. It refers to the upper class of Boston, and like it or not, I guess that's what we are, or so people tell me. Now Kelly, I want to hear everything that happened from the time you left here yesterday, even everything about Clint. Don't try to spare my feelings."

Celia walked over to her. "Marcy, are you sure you're up to this. You've had a pretty big day already."

"Yes," she said emphatically. "I may be old, and I may have been diagnosed with stage four cancer, but all of that is just words. Now that I've met my granddaughter, I've never felt better in my life. Kelly, tell me."

Kelly started with Ryan picking her up at the Portland airport and ended with Jasper picking Megan and her up at the Boston airport. Marcy listened to everything, devoid of emotion. When Kelly was finished she turned to Celia and said in a clear commanding voice, "I want you to call William and ask him to come over here right now. I want to draw up a new will. Tell him to bring whatever he has to bring in order to print it up right here and now. I want to sign it yet today, so ask him to bring a couple of witnesses."

"Marcy, can't that wait until tomorrow morning? Like I said earlier, this has been one of the biggest days you've had in a long time," Celia said.

"Absolutely not. What if I died in my sleep tonight, and Clint inherited everything? No, I'm disinheriting him. He murdered my daughter and tried to murder my granddaughter. I can never forgive him for that. Let him get a public defender. Not a penny of my money will go to him ever again." She turned to Megan and said, "I know all of this has to be a shock for you, and it is for me as well, but I'm going to make you my principal beneficiary. Of course I'll take care of Celia and some of my other staff members, plus a few of my charities, but the bulk of my estate is going to go to you. I hope that's all right with you."

"I don't know what to say. I never came here today expecting anything. I simply wanted to meet you. I don't need your money. I'm very successful in my own profession," Megan said sitting up straighter in her chair.

"Be that as it may, it's still what I'm going to do for now. If we decide we don't like each other, I can always change it, but that's what I'm going to do. Now make an old woman happy and say, thank you, grandmother," Marcy said with a grin on her face and a twinkle in her eye.

"Thank you, grandmother," Megan said, grinning back at her.

Celia went into the other room and returned a few minutes later. "William said he was on his way."

"Good. There are advantages to paying a lawyer well over a million dollars a year. It may be an inconvenient time for him, but I had no doubt he'd come."

"Marcy, it's almost 7:00, and I took the liberty of calling Mark and asking him if he could stop by, so I could talk to him," Kelly said. "I hope you don't mind."

"Not in the least. I told you how much I like him and how sorry I was when Julie told me she was going to divorce him. We'll ask him to stay for dinner. The cook is making a prime rib dinner with all the trimmings. How much time do you think you'll need to talk with him?"

"Probably about half an hour. I'd like to talk to him in private, if you don't mind."

"Of course not. Why don't you use my study? Celia, would you make sure the lamps are turned on in there?"

"Of course," she said getting up and walking into the room across the hall. Just then the doorbell rang and they all heard the maid say, "Welcome Mr. Jensen. It's good to see you again."

"Thank you. Where is everybody?"

"They're in the drawing room. You know where it is."

They all looked up as Mark walked into the room. He took one look at Megan and his eyes went wide in disbelief. He turned to Marcy and said, "What in the world is going on? I thought Julie was dead."

"She is. This is her daughter Megan. They share a remarkable similarity, don't they? I believe Kelly told you about her."

He walked over to Megan and said, "You're just as beautiful as your mother. I'm so glad to meet you." He put his hand out and they shook hands.

"Mark, don't bother sitting down. I need to talk to you. Let's go into Marcy's study," Kelly said.

As they walked across the hall, the doorbell rang and they heard the maid say to the Logan's family attorney, "It's good to see you, sir. Mrs. Logan is waiting for you in the drawing room."

CHAPTER TWENTY-EIGHT

"Kelly, what's going on? And what are you and Megan doing here? I don't understand what's going on," Mark said as they sat down in front of a desk in the study.

"A lot has taken place since I saw you yesterday. Just listen to me, and I think it will all become clear."

She told him everything that had happened yesterday and about Clint.

"That's horrific. Poor Marcy. She doesn't deserve this. To lose your daughter and then essentially lose your son. How is she taking it?"

"Better than I would have thought. I think having a relationship with Megan is the best thing that could have happened to her right now. It may even give her a reason to live. I kind of believe that our thoughts somewhat dictate the state of our health, and if she's thinking positive thoughts, who knows, maybe the experimental drug will work and give the two of them some time together. That's not the reason I wanted you to come, though."

"Seems like plenty enough reason for me," he said.

"There's more to it. When I talked to you the night before last I didn't tell you that Marcy had given Julie a graduation gift of ten million dollars." She sat back and watched his reaction.

"Wow," he said visibly impressed. "That's a lot of money. Did she leave it to Megan?"

"No. Julie never made a new will after the two of you separated and she moved to Oregon. You are the sole beneficiary of her estate and that includes the ten million dollars. Her attorney will be getting in touch with you. You're also inheriting Julie's home in Portland, and I can tell you it's both beautiful and utterly charming. Actually, you might think about using it during the winter months when it's so miserable in Maine. I would think that ten million dollars will certainly make your financial problems regarding the Harbor House go away."

Mark sat perfectly still, clearly stunned. Kelly noticed his eyes were bright with unshed tears. "Mark, are you all right?" she asked.

"No, I'm probably not. This is all surreal. First to have Julie brought back to life in the form of her daughter, and then with a few words, someone completely eliminates the money worries that have kept me from having a good night's sleep for the past two years. Kelly, it's a lot to take in."

"I'm sure it is, but it's a done deal and completely legitimate. The attorney who will be getting in touch with you is Ryan Murphy. He's a nice guy. Of course I could be prejudiced since he saved Megan's life and my life! We probably need to go join the others, and Mrs. Logan insists you stay for dinner."

"Wait. Doesn't Megan have a legal right to that money? As Julie's daughter, I would think she'd be entitled to it."

"I wondered the same thing, but Ryan told me when a parent gives a child up for adoption, all ties are essentially cut. In other words, the child gets nothing from the biological parent and vice-versa. He said Julie's will would hold up in any court of law, and really, since Megan's an attorney and adoption law is her specialty,

I'm sure she's aware of it. One thing I haven't told you is that Megan really won't need the money. Mrs. Logan is meeting with her attorney as we speak and drawing up a new will. She's going to leave the majority of her estate to Megan and completely disinherit Clint."

"I don't know what to say. Nothing in my life could have prepared me for this moment."

"I don't think it could have prepared anyone, if that's any consolation. Let's go eat dinner."

*****

Later that night Kelly got into bed and prepared to text Mike and tell him about the events of the day. She knew he'd probably been on pins and needles all day wondering what had happened. She took her phone out of her purse and saw there was a message from Stephanie.

"Sorry you weren't here for the meeting with Sophie this afternoon. What she told me was shocking, to say the least. It turns out she flew to Norfolk on Friday, intending to murder Julie. She told me she was insanely jealous of Julie and simply freaked out. Before she left, she found a man on the Internet that lives in Norfolk who sells guns to private parties with no questions asked. Apparently that's legal under Virginia's very liberal gun control laws. She purchased a gun from him and on Saturday she attended the graduation. She went to Julie's room late that afternoon, having gotten the room number from a receptionist she bribed.

When she got to the room, the door was open, and she saw Julie lying on the floor in a pool of blood, and it looked like she'd been shot. She left immediately, drove to a nearby fast food restaurant that had a large trash bin in the back, and dropped the gun in it. Then she drove to the airport and took a late flight back to Portland.

I couldn't believe what she was telling me. I asked her why she hadn't called the police, and she told me she was sure she'd be a suspect, which probably would have been true. She said she panicked. She was so relieved when I told her Clint was the murderer.

After that we talked about her job. Sophie said she knew she could have lied to me about why she'd gone to Norfolk. She said she thought about telling me she'd flown there to talk to Julie and apologize to her for some of the things Sophie had said about her. She told me she must have lost her mind for a while, because she'd never done anything like that in her life, and the more she thought about what she'd almost done, she more she felt sick about it.

She asked me if I would give her another chance at work. Sophie said she loved her job and found it hard to believe she'd done what she did. I told her I didn't know what to do. I said on one hand I was very uncomfortable having her work for me based on what I'd seen of her the last few months. I also told her she'd been a very good employee prior to her problems with Julie. We talked for a long time, and the bottom line is I've given her another chance, and she will work directly under me. We decided we'd see how we both felt about it at the end of six months. I hope it works out. Who knows? Maybe her horoscope was right for a little while at least. You might become a believer yet! See you soon."

CHAPTER TWENTY-NINE

"Mrs. Reynolds, I'm going to miss you. What a whirlwind of things have happened at the Logan house since you first met with Mrs. Logan a few days ago."

"Thanks, Jasper. It's been quite a week, and I'm certainly looking forward to going home, playing with my dogs, and cooking for my husband before I have to get back to work. I really appreciate your texting me about Clint. Obviously your suspicions were well-grounded." She opened the door while he got her luggage out of the trunk. Kelly reached up and put her hand on his cheek. "Again, thanks for everything. You take care of everyone." She turned and walked into the terminal.

Six hours later she walked out the arrival door at the Portland Airport and saw Liz waving to her. She walked over to Liz's car, put her luggage in the back seat, and said, "Thanks again for picking me up. I think I owe you big time. One round trip to the Portland Airport from Cedar Bay is a big deal. Two round trips are above and beyond friendship."

"I probably wouldn't do it for just anyone, but given what you've done for Doc and me, consider the debt being paid in increments. Mike filled me in on what happened in Boston, and even though it was emotional it sounds like it went well."

Liz was a psychologist, so she was always interested in emotional issues. "Liz, I would say it went beyond well. When I left this morning, Megan and Marcy were practically beaming with pleasure at being together. I don't know what the future holds for either of them, but it seems to be a lot better than the past."

"Kelly, they all owe you a huge debt of gratitude. If it hadn't been for you, this never would have happened."

"Who knows? I'm just glad I had a chance to play a role in all of it. Now, if I can get Mike up to Maine to the Harbor House and take advantage of the cottage Mark said I could always stay in for free, then it really would be worthwhile."

"I wouldn't complain. You've been to Cuba and Italy recently. That's not too shabby for a woman who'd barely made it out of Oregon prior to marrying Mike."

"That's true, but now that I've had a taste of travel, I've gotten to like it. I'll have to think of somewhere else to go. Actually, I'd kind of like to go to Spain. I've always been fascinated by the country, and I could learn how to make some Spanish food I could serve at the coffee shop. Wouldn't that be nice?"

"Why don't you just sit back and relax?" Liz said. "You might even try to close your eyes. Rather imagine with everything that's happened recently you're probably sleep deprived and don't even know it.

"Think I'll take you up on that," Kelly said as she closed her eyes and was soon dreaming of Spanish food and Michelin starred restaurants.

EPILOGUE

One morning a month later, Kelly's phone rang. "This is Kelly Reynolds."

"Kelly, I'm glad you answered. It's Megan Simmons. I had some business in Portland, and if you're going to be home around noon, I'd like to drive down and talk to you."

"I'd love it. I've wondered how everything went after I left Boston. See you at noon. Plan on lunch. I'll come up with something."

Kelly looked down at the three furry bodies standing at her feet eagerly wagging their tails, and letting her know they'd like a little attention. "Sorry, guys. I need to come up with something for lunch. Maybe Megan will pay some attention to you when she gets here."

Two hours later she put the finishing touches on the Caesar salads she'd made which were topped with sliced chicken. She turned the oven on for the biscuits and made a large pitcher of iced tea. For dessert she'd prepared a sauce with fresh blueberries which she planned to serve over vanilla bean ice cream. Since it was just the two of them, Kelly decided to eat in the kitchen, so she set the kitchen table with placemats and napkins in bright summery colors. When she heard Megan's car pull into the driveway she put the biscuits in the oven.

Momentarily there was a knock on the door, and she hurried to open it. Megan was standing there with the largest bouquet of pink roses Kelly had ever seen. She gasped and said, "What is this?"

"This is my way of saying thank you," Megan said as she walked into the house, handed Kelly the bouquet, and hugged her. "Where are those adorable dogs I never got to play with the last time I was here?"

"They're in the back yard. You can let them in while I find a vase large enough to hold this bouquet."

A few moments later Megan was on the floor, trying to give belly rubs to three dogs that were whimpering with delight. She stood up and said, "Later, guys. I need to talk to Kelly right now."

"Megan, why don't you sit down at the kitchen table? Let me dress the salads, and by the time I'm finished with that the biscuits should be done." She put the pitcher of iced tea on the table and poured Megan a glass. A minute later Kelly sat down at the table and joined her.

"So tell me everything. What happened after I left Boston?"

Megan took a bite of salad and broke off a piece of her biscuit. "This is delicious, Kelly. Thanks."

"Glad you like it. Start with when I left."

"All right," Megan said. "I spent the rest of the weekend at the Logan House and flew back to Portland on Sunday night. Kelly, my grandmother is simply incredible. You'd given me the Logan Family History book, and she and I spent a lot of time going over it, so I could get a sense of who everyone was in the family. She's one of the smartest people I've ever met, and I have to say really brave."

"Did she talk about Clint?" Kelly asked.

"Yes. She said sometimes there's just a bad seed in a family, and she felt he was that bad seed. Grandmother told me she'd felt guilty for years, blaming herself for Clint's behavior and that somehow she was responsible for the way he'd turned out. Given the fact he murdered my mother and tried to murder you and me absolved her of any further thoughts and feelings of guilt about her relationship with Clint. She said she may have made mistakes in her life, but she never made one as bad as her failure to recognize and accept the fact that Clint was simply rotten to the core. Actually, I think it's a very healthy way for her to look at the situation."

"How are the two you getting along?"

"That's what I came to talk to you about. I'm moving to Boston, and I'm going to take the Massachusetts State Bar. There are only a handful of attorneys in the area who specialize in adoption law, and I think I can do very well there. The fact that grandmother's attorney is the senior partner in the most prestigious law firm in Boston probably won't hurt, plus he's already told me I can have an office and a job at his firm after I pass the bar."

"That's wonderful! I'll bet Marcy is thrilled."

"I think she is. As a matter of fact, I'll be living in the Logan House. I was reluctant to do that, but she said that house is so big I can have my own floor, so it would be like having my own house. I thought about it and couldn't find a reason not to do it, plus it's close to the law firm and very close to the downtown area. If anyone had told me a few weeks ago my life would change like this, I wouldn't have believed it, and I owe it all to you."

"I wish I could take credit for your good fortune, but I just kind of put one foot in front of the other, and it simply ended up the way it did. I'm really happy for you. Have you seen Mark?"

"Yes, actually he and I have become quite close. I feel I know my mother much better because of all he's told me about her, and certainly he has a different perspective on her than Grandmother."

"Yes, I would imagine he does. I like him a lot. Have you been up to the Harbor House?" Kelly asked.

"I have, and I love it up there. Mark told me I'm always welcome, and with the money he's going to receive, he's planning on adding two new cottages. Although he hasn't said anything, I think he must be doing much better. I've been there twice and each time there were no vacancies, and the restaurant was full from the time it opened until the time it closed.

"Please do me a favor when you return to Boston. Give my best to Mrs. Logan, Celia, Mark, and even Jasper. They were all wonderful to me."

"I will." She looked at her watch. "I need to get back to Portland and then fly to San Francisco. The moving van is going to be there tomorrow, and I don't want to cut it too close." She stood up and walked over to Kelly, hugging her. "Kelly, I can never thank you enough. Because of you, I have a completely new life. Thank you, thank you, thank you!"

"Be happy, Megan, just be happy. You deserve it."

As she closed the door behind Megan, she thought once again that life really was stranger than fiction. Who could have scripted the events of the last month?

RECIPES

SHE CRAB SOUP

Ingredients:
1 lb. lump crabmeat, divided (If you can get fresh crab, it's better, but if you're like most of us, it's going to have to be canned. Just make sure it's lump crab meat, not some imitation crab meat.)
1 large onion, finely diced
1 bay leaf
2 tbsp. garlic, minced
2 tbsp. butter
2 tbsp. flour
2 cups crab stock (Good luck getting that! I've used fish stock when I could find it, and if not, I've found that chicken stock works well.)
2 cups milk (I know some of you use 2% or skim, but I like whole milk in this. Yes, it's rich, but that's part of what makes it so good.)
1 ½ cups heavy cream (Said it was rich!)
2 tsp. paprika
½ cup dry sherry wine
½ cup crab roe, divided (Once again, good luck! It does give the soup a nice red-orange color, but I think it's close to impossible to find, unless you live on the East Coast, but if you can find it, use it.)

Salt and pepper to taste
2 tbsp. chopped chives
1 tsp. Worcestershire sauce
Splash of dry white wine (I use a lot of wine in cooking. Think it makes things taste better, but if you choose not to, it's not going to ruin the dish!)
Squeeze of lemon juice
Dash of hot sauce

Directions:

Melt 2 tablespoons butter in a large heavy-bottomed saucepan over medium heat. Add the onion, garlic, and bay leaf, and lightly sauté for 2 minutes. Sprinkle the flour in and stir to coat. Whisk in the stock until the mixture is lump free. Gradually add the milk, cream, paprika, 2 tablespoons of sherry, Worcestershire sauce, hot sauce, wine, and the squeeze of lemon, stirring constantly for 2 more minutes.

Remove contents from the heat, transfer to a blender, and blend. Return the blended mixture back to the pan. Add half the crab meat and if you've been lucky, the roe. Season with salt and pepper to taste. Simmer for 10 minutes, stirring until it's thick and blended.

Divide the remaining sherry and crab meat among four bowls. Ladle the hot soup over the crab meat and sherry. Garnish with chopped chives. I like to serve this with warm crusty French bread. Enjoy!

APPLE CRISP WITH TOPPING

Ingredients:
6 apples, peeled, cored, and diced
2 tbsp. white sugar
½ tsp. ground cinnamon (Freshly ground is lovely, but if you don't have it, you can use prepared.)
9" square glass pan (If you only have a round one, that's fine.)

Topping Ingredients:
1 cup brown sugar (I prefer light brown sugar.)
¾ cup rolled oats
¾ cup all-purpose flour
1 tsp. ground cinnamon
½ cup cold butter
Whipped cream (You can make it yourself or use canned whipped cream if you're short on time, but I think freshly made is ever so much better!)

Directions:
Preheat oven to 350 degrees. Toss apples with white sugar and ½ tsp. cinnamon to coat. Spoon into a 9" square glass baking pan.

Mix brown sugar, oats, flour, and 1 tsp. cinnamon in a separate bowl. Use two forks or a pastry cutter to mash the butter into the oat mixture until it resembles coarse crumbs. Spread evenly over the apples and pat down gently.

Bake in preheated oven for 40 minutes or until golden brown. Cool for about ten minutes. Cut into pieces, plate, and put a dollop of whipped cream on top. Enjoy!

LOBSTER ROLLS

Ingredients:
1 ½ lbs. cooked lobster meat chopped into bite-size pieces (Fresh lobster meat from lobster tails or claws is preferable, but it you don't live where it's available, pre-packaged will do.)
4 top slit hot dog buns
½ cup mayonnaise
3 tbsp. freshly squeezed lemon juice
Salt and fresh ground pepper to taste
2 celery stalks, finely chopped (I like to use the ones from inside the celery bundle. I think they're more tender.)

Directions:
Combine the lobster meat, mayonnaise, celery, salt, and pepper in a bowl. (I like to let the flavors marry for about thirty minutes in the

refrigerator before serving.)

Pull the sides of the hot dog buns apart, but don't completely split them. Fill each roll with ¼ of the mixture. Enjoy!

BOSTON CREAM PIE

Ingredients:

Cream Filling:
1 ½ cups whole milk
2 large egg yolks
1/3 cup white sugar
2 tbsp. cornstarch
1/8 tsp. salt
2 tsp. vanilla (Don't skimp on costs and use imitation. You can taste the difference!)
Plastic wrap

Cake:
Baking spray & 2 tbsp. flour to prepare pan
1 ¼ cups all-purpose flour or 1 ½ cups cake flour
1/3 cup butter
¾ cup whole milk
¾ cup sugar
1 ½ tsp. baking powder
1 tsp. vanilla
½ tsp. salt
1 large egg
Rubber spatula
9" round cake pan
(Truth be told, I have substituted a yellow cake mix or even bought a yellow cake at the supermarket when I was tight on time, although I think "from scratch" is always preferable. Let your schedule be your guide!)

Chocolate Icing:

3 oz. unsweetened baking chocolate
3 – 4 tbsp. water
1 cup powdered sugar, sifted
¾ tsp. vanilla
1 glass measuring cup

Filling Directions:

Place the yolks in a bowl and beat with a fork until mixed. Stir in 1 ½ cups milk and set aside.

In a medium saucepan stir ½ cup sugar, cornstarch, and 1/8 tsp. salt until mixed. Gradually stir the egg mixture in. Cook over medium heat, stirring constantly, until it thickens and boils. Boil for 1 minute and remove from heat. Stir in 2 tsp. vanilla. Cover the top with a sheet of plastic wrap to prevent a tough layer from forming. Refrigerate at least 2 hours. It will hold up to 24 hours in the refrigerator.

Cake:

Preheat the oven to 350 degrees. Prepare a 9" round cake pan with spray and flour, tapping out the excess flour. Combine cake ingredients in a bowl and beat with an electric beater for 30 seconds on low speed. Scrape sides from time to time with a rubber spatula. Pour the mixture into the prepared pan and smooth the top of the batter. Bake about 35 minutes or until a toothpick inserted in the center comes out clean. Cool cake in the pan on a cooling rack for 30 minutes. Remove cake from pan and keep it on the cooling rack for one hour.

Chocolate Icing:

In a small saucepan melt 3 tbsp. of butter and the chocolate over a low heat, stirring occasionally. Microwave the water in a glass measuring cup until hot, 15 – 30 seconds. Remove chocolate mixture from heat, whisk in the powdered sugar and ¾ tsp. vanilla. Stir in 3 tbsp. of water. Stir in additional water, 1 tsp. at a time as needed, until the icing is smooth and thin enough to spread.

Assembly:

Split the cake horizontally. Place the bottom layer on a serving plate, cut side up. Spread filling over bottom layer. Place the top of the cake on the filling, cut side down.

Using the back of a spoon or a frosting knife, spread the icing over the top of the cake, allowing some to drizzle down the sides. Refrigerate uncovered. Slice into pie-shaped pieces, plate, and enjoy!

Pasta with Seafood and Fra Diavolo (Brother Devil) Sauce

Seafood:
8 oz. scallops
8 oz. large shrimp, peeled and deveined
8 oz. mussels
8 oz. clams
(I like to prepare this dish with fresh seafood, but I realize this may be a problem for some of you. It's usually pretty easy to get frozen shrimp and scallops, but clams and mussels may not be available. If not, use a large can, 16 oz., of whole baby clams and forget the mussels. I made it that way a few nights ago, and it was delicious!)

Sauce Ingredients:
4 tbsp. olive oil, divided
6 garlic cloves, finely chopped
3 cups canned chopped peeled tomatoes, with liquid
1 ½ tsp. salt
1 tsp. crushed red pepper flakes
16 oz. package linguine

Directions:
In a large saucepan, heat 2 tbsp. olive oil. Add garlic. Cook for one minute and stir in tomatoes and liquid. Season with salt and red pepper. Bring to a boil, lower the heat, and simmer for 30 minutes. If

using fresh clams and mussels, put them in the last ten minutes. (If they don't open after ten minutes, toss them. They might be bad.)

Meanwhile bring a large pot of salted water to a boil (It literally should taste like the ocean.) Cook pasta for 8 to 10 minutes, depending on package instructions.

In a large skillet heat the remaining 1 tbsp. of olive oil over high heat. Add the shrimp and scallops and cook for about 2 – 3 minutes. (Caution! Don't overcook them, because they'll taste rubbery.) Add them to the tomato mixture and turn up the heat to medium high. If using canned clams, add them now. Cook for about 4 minutes. Serve the sauce over the cooked linguini and enjoy!

Kindle & Ebooks for FREE

Go to www.dianneharman.com/freepaperback.html and get your FREE copies of Dianne's books and Dianne's favorite recipes immediately by signing up for her newsletter.

Once you've signed up for her newsletter you're eligible to win a Kindle. One lucky winner is picked every week. Hurry before the offer ends.

ABOUT THE AUTHOR

Dianne lives in Huntington Beach, California, with her husband, Tom, a former California State Senator, and her boxer dog, Kelly. Her passions are cooking, reading, and dogs, so whenever she has a little free time, you can either find her in the kitchen, playing with Kelly in the back yard, or curled up with the latest book she's reading.

Her award winning books include:

Cedar Bay Cozy Mystery Series
Kelly's Koffee Shop, Murder at Jade Cove, White Cloud Retreat, Marriage and Murder, Murder in the Pearl District, Murder in Calico Gold, Murder at the Cooking School, Murder in Cuba, Trouble at the Kennel, Murder on the East Coast

Liz Lucas Cozy Mystery Series
Murder in Cottage #6, Murder & Brandy Boy, The Death Card, Murder at The Bed & Breakfast, The Blue Butterfly, Murder at the Big T Lodge

High Desert Cozy Mystery Series
Murder & The Monkey Band, Murder & The Secret Cave, Murdered by Country Music

Midwest Cozy Mystery Series
Murdered by Words

Jack Trout Cozy Mystery Series
Murdered in Argentina

Coyote Series
Blue Coyote Motel, Coyote in Provence, Cornered Coyote

Website: www.dianneharman.com
Blog: www.dianneharman.com/blog
Email: dianne@dianneharman.com

Newsletter
If you would like to be notified of her latest releases please go to www.dianneharman.com and sign up for her newsletter.

Made in the USA
Monee, IL
09 November 2022

17441619R00100